Deep Overstock

#15: Shakespeare
January 2022

" Now we sit through Shakespeare in order to **"**
recognize the quotations.

Orson Welles

DRAMA - SHAKESPEARE

Editorial

Editors-In-Chief: Mickey Collins & Robert Eversmann

Managing Editors: Michael Santiago & Z.B. Wagman

Poetry: Jihye Shin

Prose: Michael Santiago & Z.B. Wagman

Copyeditor: A.G. Angevine

Cover: *The First Appearance of William Shakespeare on the Stage of the Globe Theatre*, George Cruikshank, 1864-1865

Contact: editors@deepoverstock.com
deepoverstock.com

ON THE SHELVES

COMEDIES

9 "The Merry Real Housewives of Windsor" and Other Modern Shakespearean Adaptations by Jen Mierisch

12 On Appointing a Committee Chairperson: a Golden Shovel Poem by Wilda Morris

13 Yarrow Spells by James Hall

14 Shakespeare Imprisoned by Dr. Thomas Davison

18 Emilia at the Curtain by Elizabeth Sylvia

21 Ringed by Elizabeth Sylvia

22 VIOLA'S SONG by Kathryn Paulsen

23 The Hag in the Tree by Kate Falvey

25 Quoting Scripture: a Snake Poem by Wilda Morris

26 Prospero & Company Go Way Off Book by John Sullivan

42 Even Shakespeare Knew, a Mesostic Poem by Wilda Morris

43 A Bard in the Forest of Arden by Kate Falvey

45 Dear Helena, by Elizabeth Sylvia

47 Antonio's Waves: (A meditation on Twelfth Night) by Nicholas Yandell

50 Bottom by Frank De Canio

TRAGEDIES

53 shakespeare zombie by RC deWinter

54 Weird Sisters by Elizabeth Sylvia

55 A Carving by James B. Nicola

56 Iago Resides Inside the Insane Asylum by John Davis

57 A POUND OF FLESH by Roy Schreiber

66 To My Last Syllable by Debbie Peters

67 Ophelia by Ed Higgins

68 Ode to Cordelia by Shakti Pada Mukhopadhyay

69 Sonnet At Last by Teresa Sari FitzPatrick

70 A Short Summary of the Aubade from Romeo and Juliet Act 3, Scene 5 by David de Young

71 Parsing #3 by Karla Linn Merrifield

continued...

continued...

72 A Shakespearean curse by Timothy Arliss OBrien

73 Weirds to Stage by Anna Laura Falvey

74 Mercutio's Lament by Valerie Hunter

76 Shakespeare Did Not Know How My Mother Would Die: a Trimeric Poem by Wilda Morris

77 SHAKESPEARE'S GHOST by Kathryn Paulsen

78 Ophelia Laughs by Kate Falvey

79 Night is Over and Day is Almost Here by Z.B. Wagman

87 Her Peacock Feathers (as a Montague antagonist) by Frank De Canio

Histories

91 Understudy by Elizabeth Sylvia

93 Cordelia's Wisdom for Today by Wilda Morris

94 Elevator Macbeth by Maev Barba

103 Calpurnia's Speech after Caesar's Death by Chaitra Kotasthane

105 Antony Wrestles with His Love for Cleopatra: a Cento by Wilda Morris

106 Slow as the Elephant by Elizabeth Sylvia

Problems

109 The Eternal by K.B. Thomas

111 When Shakespeare Wrote a Haiku by Lynette G. Esposito

112 A Bard and his Shadow by Bogdan Groza

116 Words Are Lies -- Magical Antidote #2 by Farnilf P.

118 A Feral Cat Named Shakespeare by Lynette G. Esposito

119 Shakespeare Replies to Attacks on Theatre by Greg Bell

121 Palinode: Shakespeare's Women by Elizabeth Sylvia

122 Me by A.G. Angevine

123 You by A.G. Angevine

124 The Bard Cowboy by Lynette G. Esposito

Letter from the Editors

Dearest Readers,

What light through yonder journal breaks? It's the 15th issue of Deep Overstock: Shakespeare! We could bardly contain ourselves while reading all of your submissions.

This issue we have pieces that are Comedies, Tragedies, and Histories, and Problem Plays, just like the great playwright himself. We've got Ophelias, Caesars, Juliets, Antonys, Hamlets, hags, and witches. What a super cast of characters.

Speaking of super characters, submissions for Issue 16: Superheroes are open from now until February 28th. Up, up, and away, dear readers!

Yours, until the curtain falls,

Deep Overstock Editors

COMEDIES

"Virginity breeds mites, much like a cheese."

All's Well That Ends Well, Act 1, Scene 1

"The Merry Real Housewives of Windsor" and Other Modern Shakespearean Adaptations

by Jen Mierisch

English teachers, do you despair of helping students connect with the classics? Are they more interested in TikTok and Insta than Troilus and Cressida? Show them these modern adaptations, brought to you in iambic pentameter by Fakespeare Productions. In two shakes of a knight's codpiece, your teens will sound as educated as Elizabethan peasants!

1. The Taming of the Screen Time

In this lighthearted romp (a sequel to "404 Page Not Found: A Comedy of Errors"), Peter attempts a series of stunts to persuade the reluctant Kate to love him more than she loves her smartphone.

Peter:

> 'Tis simpler, squeezing nectar from a stone,
> Than winning thy attention from thy phone!

Kate:

> How now, dear Pete! What makes thee so uptight?
> I used this very tool to swipe thee right!

2. Hamless, the Vegan Prince of Denmark

In this tragic tale, Claudius, CEO of Elsinore Pharma, marries Prince Hamlet's widowed mother, Gertrude. Hamlet's father's ghost tells Hamlet he was poisoned by tainted beef. Distraught, Hamlet reads obsessively about bovine growth hormones and swears off animal products. His concerned girlfriend, Ophelia, tries to tempt him with freshly cooked bacon, but he rejects her, declaring that henceforth he shall be called Hamless. Events escalate when Hamless hijacks a slideshow of Claudius and Gertrude's honeymoon photos to play videos from "truther" conspiracy theorists.

Hamless:

> Alas, poor Yorick! I knew him, Horatio.
> I wager he died of poisoned poultry, ho!

Horatio:

> But Yorick's end was plain to all with eyes.
> He choked on bread and thus met his demise.

Hamless:

> Friend, wake up, seek truth, be not a sheep.
> Big Pharma wants you dumb and e'er asleep.

3. The Merry Real Housewives of Windsor

In Season 2 of this television dramedy, notorious gigolo John Falstaff visits Windsor, looking for backers for his tech startup. As Falstaff presses the flesh at society parties, Mrs. Page and Mrs. Ford complain about him to their fellow housewives. They declare that there's only one thing worse than a male cheapskate (like last season's guest, Tight-Ass Andronicus): a male gold-digger. When Falstaff sends lewd text messages to both women, attempting to seduce cash out of them, they orchestrate a series of pranks to get revenge.

Mrs. Page:

> 'Tis not enough to take our husbands' gold;
> This villain thinks that *we'll* be bought and sold?
> His swollen ego, loosed by some magician,
> Could swallow up this town like Wandavision!

Mrs. Ford:

> Fear not, dear Page, and ne'er admit defeat,

For we shall be the death of his conceit.
See here, my hidden camera in the hickory.
By my troth, the world shall see his trickery!

4. Two Gentlemansplainers of Verona

In this Netflix miniseries, two buddies from Verona, N.J., Vinny and Pablo, piss off their girlfriends, Julia and May, after the boys jokingly present a feminine perspective on dating. Facing a boring summer with no girls, the boys accept a trip to Milan with Vinny's rich uncle Bruno. There, they meet local babes Sylvia and Veronica (actually Julia in disguise), who school them in how to properly respect a woman.

Vinny:

> 'Tis true, my utterance may have been unwise.
> But oh, that May is candy for the eyes!

Sylvia:

> Sir, you shall die a poor frustrated satyr,
> Until you love her mind over her matter.

> #

Enjoyed Fakespeare? Don't miss the modern 19th-century classic about a single woman who freezes her eggs: *Madame Ovary*.

On Appointing a Committee Chairperson: a Golden Shovel Poem
by Wilda Morris

"Better a witty fool than a foolish wit."
~ William Shakespeare, *Twelfth Night*

Tell me, friend, which you think makes a better
chair: a teacher or a lawyer, a welder or a
cook? A sober woman or a drunken man who's witty?
Someone who asks no pity and knows himself a fool
or someone ghoulish who thinks himself much wiser than
the rest of the committee, insists on leading a
new project everyone finds foolish,
one whose brain is itty-bitty, lacking judgment, lacking wit?

Yarrow Spells
by James Hall

Spells inspired by *Midsummer's Nights Dream*

Love Medicine

> Yarrow blossom sparkles like the sun,
> rayed white flowers, spirit powers
> anoint sleeping lids with potion fine
> awakened at dawn, loves eyes meet
> mine. His heart, I snare, with yarrow fair
> More lustrous appears my hair,
> more alluring becomes my face,
> ardor enraptured by my grace.
> Capture soul, my love for me alone,
> each kiss, his soul I will devour,
>   Desire naught save honeyed lips,
> all other loves I will eclipse,
> passion flame captured for only one,
> if he loves me not, let him love none.

Healing

> Yarrow, may I be the morning star at dawn,
> Yarrow, make me a rock for clan to rest on,
> Yarrow, use me as a staff to bear the weak,
> Yarrow, cast me true portent reading,
> Yarrow, stop injured wounds bleeding,
> Yarrow, strengthen my power to heal.
> Yarrow, restore my energy,
>   Then, no one will ever wound me.

Shakespeare Imprisoned
by Dr. Thomas Davison

From the author: After five years of teaching inside two all-male State Prisons in Northern Ohio, I know first-hand the power of Shakespeare and poetry. Like other art forms, poetry is universal in its appeal. Shakespeare remains a source of powerful lessons. Sure, I have an expensive doctorate, and if you hold my feet to the fire, I could quote the similarities between Shakespeare's iambic pentameter and hip-hop music. Despite the opinions of the prison hierarchy that "*Felons would never embrace and benefit from Shakespeare or poetry.*" It wasn't "*a waste of my time and theirs*" and they were not "*incapable of learning anything of value from Shakespeare.*" Read the following true story and judge for yourselves.

"That's not *another* poem you're gonna read to us is it Doctor D.?" asked the blue denim-clad inmate in a strident voice?

"Why yes it certainly is Mr. Jones" I replied calmly as I took the stack of offending photocopies from a plastic see-through container. The same container that I was required to use when carrying any of my teaching materials into Merrytown (name changed) Correctional Institution (MCI), an all-male prison in northern Ohio. "Why Mr. Jones I thought you enjoyed the poetry I bring inside," I asked with a soft chuckle. "Aren't you the gentleman who asked me for extra copies of *The Rose That Grew in Concrete* to share with your bunkies?" I queried with a broad smile.

"Yea, that was me Doctor D., but that was Tupac Shakur, he's cool." He paused and looked around the room to ensure his peers and fellow students weren't paying close attention. "Last time you brought in that Shakespeare dude." He hesitated then blurted. "He's been dead for like a thousand years," he stated with an exasperated sigh. "And the time before that it was Kipling, also dead forever."

"Alright, Mr. Jones fair enough." I turned and faced the entire classroom. "Let's review shall we?" I cleared my throat loudly to get the attention of the entire class and stated in a loud firm voice, "Class, I have another poem with me today that I want to share with the class." I heard a couple of groans.

Mr. Jones, who secretly liked poetry (but was concerned it might not be perceived as manly to do so), squawked in a shrill voice, "Not again!"

I knew that this objection was for the benefit of his peers, but I felt it was time to call him on it. "Alright class, who can tell me the quote from the character in the Murakami story about books? Anyone?" A burly tattooed inmate who always sat in the front row and took copious notes raised his well-muscled arm. "Yes, Mr. Jackson, what was the quote in question?"

Without any hesitation, Mr. Jackson responded in a deep booming baritone, "If you only read the books that everyone else is reading you can only think what everyone else is thinking - Haruki Murakami."

I nodded with enthusiasm. "Very good. And what does that quote mean to you, Mr. Jackson?"

Again, without slowing his response, "It's like you are always telling us sir, we are college students now we have to learn critical thinking, challenge everything, question everything. One way to do this is by reading things outside of our comfort zone." Mr. Jackson smiled at me and his classmates "That is how you probably discovered Tupac, Doctor D. We know you love your poetry." He finished with his statement with an even broader smile directed at all of us.

From the back of the room Mr. Brown (an informal class leader) spoke out, "Yea, Doctor D. is always bringing in those classic books and all that philosopher stuff cause he wants us to think for ourselves!" He gave me a supportive nod of his head.

"Very good gentlemen." I returned Mr. Brown's nod with one of my own. I continued, "Last week I brought in an excerpt from *The Merchants of Venice* by William Shakespeare." I shot Mr. Jones a hard stare when I said the word Shakespeare. "Can anyone tell me what they learned from that one?" I saw several hands raised, including Mr. Washington's who normally was very introverted. I said in a softer voice, "Mr. Washington, your thoughts on this matter?"

He spoke so quietly that everyone strained to hear him. "Well sir, we were talking about bias and prejudice and that excerpt we discussed was about a Jew from like 500 years ago. I really liked that one," he mumbled. He hesitated for a moment and then in a much louder voice, "I remember these parts best 'Hath, not a Jew's eyes?' 'Hath not a Jew hands?' And uh, 'fed with the same food, hurt with the same weapons.' And oh yea, also my favorite part, 'If you prick us do we not bleed? If you tickle us do we not laugh? If you poison us do we not die?' " Now there wasn't a sound in the room as he finished his impromptu speech. "I believe that you were trying to show us that bias has been around forever sir, that it is a part of human nature and to try to keep it in perspective when you personally experience it. Well anyway," his voice trailed off. "That's the message I got."

Still waters run deep, I thought to myself. These incarcerated students never cease to amaze me. "Very good Mr. Washington, very, very good!"

"And finally gentlemen what about the poem *IF* by Rudyard Kipling." As I was speaking I was striding briskly toward where Mr. Jones was seated. I purposely stopped directly in front of his seat and locked my eyes with his. "What about it Mr. Jones, you have heard from your classmates, now it's your turn. What did you get from the Kipling poem?"

Mr. Jones's eyes wandered away from my intence stare. He looked around the room and realized that everyone was watching him, waiting for his response. "Well uh, in class we were talking about the characteristics of a good leader and father, and uh what skills we will need to succeed when we get out of this place and back to the real world." He paused as he formulated his next words. "The Kipling poem spoke about the things we were talking about in class such as (being lied about but don't deal in lies) that was the characteristic of honesty. And then there was the part about (to serve your turn long after they are gone) well that was integrity." He paused for another moment and finished his thoughts with, "Uh ok I liked the ending the best" in a voice so soft that everyone was leaning forward in their seats to make out his words. "Yours is the Earth and everything that's in it, And which is more you'll be a man, my son!" He sighed heavily.

    I leaned down to be inches from his face and said to him, "Excellent job Mr. Jones, absolutely excellent." He smiled at me.

    I marched quickly back to my desk, scooped up the stack of 35 photocopies, and placed them squarely in front of Mr. Jones. "Will you be so kind as to distribute this week's poem for me, Mr. Jones, please?" I asked him as I made my way to the old chalk blackboard that was in the front of my prison classroom.

    "Yes sir!" I heard enthusiastically from behind me as I began writing in chalk on the ancient board.

    I took a moment and allowed myself a broad smile. Despite all the naysaying from my teaching peers what I thought I knew had been proven true poetry was universal! I continued to talk to my class of incarcerated students gathered behind me. "Today we have an excerpt called All the World's a Stage from the play *As You Like It* which is written by Mr. Jones's favorite author Willy Shakespeare. Oscar Wilde stated 'All the world is a wtage, but the play was badly cast.' What did he mean by that, I wonder? Remember our discussion about the power of metaphors as a useful leadership tool? Remember our discussion about *Lion King* and the circle of life?" I paused writing and turned and flashed a sheepish grin. "I remember how the entire class, including me, admitted to really liking that movie! Well, Shakespeare wrote his own version of the circle of life metaphor hundreds of years ago. He called it the Seven Ages of Man. Okay class, let us begin."

Emilia at the Curtain
by Elizabeth Sylvia

Descend. Be stone no more.
— The Winter's Tale
"Was Shakespeare a Woman?"
— Elizabeth Winkler, The Atlantic

Remember, when absence comes along
ringing his empty bell of doubt
that everyone will someday dream about
the loves they lost and those they left among

the ruins when the bonds
they built in bed were broken
by the stricter social rules (spoken
and not) that say a man must respond

to jealousy or pregnancy with equal
aversion and shuttle off the woman,
who has revealed her monstrous form
before his eyes so all her secret

charms shatter on the floor, to death
or banishment. Take Emilia Bassano, whom
some scholars have looked to
name Shakespeare's Dark Lady, with

her brunette hair, her foreign
skin, her Italian musicality,
her well-read intellectual vitality.
All unusual enough that she became

the first English woman to publish
a book of her own verse and seek
for patronage, and so unique
that some would establish

her as the true author of the plays
(see: Elizabeth Winkler, writing in *The Atlantic*,

on the controversy around that dramatic
provenance), an argument that reappraises

the rich development of female
characters as feminist imagination
on the Tudor stage, the insinuation
being that Emilia railed

against the restrictions of her sex and life
in Shakespeare's name. Did she put
herself in every blameless heroine who lets
a fake demise resolve the strife

her witless husband puts her through?
Emilia adored her life at court, but when
her lover Henry Carey, the Baron
of Hudson impregnated her, he shooed

her out and made her by marriage
an exile from all the glitter and wit
she loved. Her whole existence closeted
shamed small forgotten wreckage

to the Baron, but for Emilia, curtained
like Hermione in the *The Winter's Tale*,
hope that memory would soften to recall
her, to breathe love once again

into the statue of her day, so that she
could step down from the endless waiting
and grasp the hand of life, persuading
everyone with her forgiveness and beauty,

her poetry and song, to take her back
and set her high on the only stage
that mattered, where courtiers arranged
language to pleasure, refracted

one another's novelty, and delights like
sugar cakes were plentiful. In the plays
this happens often, but in Emilia's
life there was no Act V,

only miscarriages and poverty,
the husband who disparaged her
and sold her jewels, unheralded work,
the hopeless wish for sovereignty

over one's own days and reputation,
for control of pen, body and mind
instead of the convent/casket/closet designed
to trap female humanity in its low station.

Ringed
by Elizabeth Sylvia

All that was mine in Silvia I give thee –Two Gentlemen of Verona

How to make a woman mute:
Give her to your friend like the object
of affection she always was.

In Shakespeare, lovers are always
trading rings, each one the licked
fingerprint of a beloved, an arrow
to the eye of the faithless.

Turn the ring sideways and it shows
the hollow of a lover's heart, the space
his finger forgets to occupy as soon
as that slim first vow is out of sight.

There are two women in *Two Gentlemen*,
and one ring passed between them:

Julia gives it to her love, but he
gives it to Silvia, who loves
his friend instead. When Silvia
won't take the ring, her lover
proffers Silvia's whole self instead.

Silvia never speaks a word again
in the whole play, her mouth
an empty O, her body a space
ready for slipping on.

In comedy, men bound
without a rebound,
and women, knowing love
must be a secret or a shame,
go on holding, strung around
their necks or deep in pocket,
the ring of remembrance,
the empty *me-men-to*.

VIOLA'S SONG
by Kathryn Paulsen

Fair ones change their skins to change their songs.
Dare you shed false love to mate true peer?
Give your heart, as hard as art is long?

Poor tunes assail you; still you say, play on!
Finer melodies shall scale your ear.
Fair ones change their skins to change their songs.

Cast away these shards of fancied wrongs.
Play lays that last the length of love's fast year.
Give your heart, as hard as art is long.

Love's not blind: unbind it from snake's prong.
In strange guise you'll find a rare kin near.
Fair ones change their skins to change their songs.

Feed on your servant till your heart stirs, strong.
Learn harmonies from her you cannot hear.
Give your heart, as hard as art is long.

Live dangerously—and lie where you belong.
Dare to win true friend—love's music share.
Fair ones change their skins to change their song.
Lose your heart, as hard as art is long.

The Hag in the Tree
by Kate Falvey

I crept up to him while he slept
and studied the twitches his dreams made
beneath his frail eyelids. He should
have sensed my stare.

Soon I knew if he
was being chased by wings and needles,
or if he was lost in a flailing bark
inside the snapping prongs of foreign waves.

I took a shine to his beauty
and studied his wavy gouts of silent pain,
shirred through the pine bark I'd made
from my own withered skin.

I crept in after filling my son
with the riot of the moon
and teaching him the languages
of spindrift: light, and growth, and change.

This little slip of a sprite in the pine
knew nothing but delicate abandon,
weak-willed hostility, monstrous self-
regard, his magic imprecise and wanton.

He played havoc with my infant son
tormenting for flimsy pleasure with a
slippery and ephemeral power. I spied
him poisoning a flower, discerned

his plans to tease my son to brinks
of docility and dread, shrinking him
to meager genuflection, the son of
Setebos and Sycorax! the leashed

hound of a smirking sprite,
the least of all the voices on

our isle, the bare whim of a noise,
a poser, a mothy flirt of minor arrogance.

And yet, this ambiguous he
in my tree calls me to a dangerous
maternal softness, vying with maternal
rage. My son must be ascendant

but the world, being a stage,
requires antagonists and will slip
into mazy wanderings that even I
cannot control, despite my art,

despite my ancient vanity, despite
my incandescent age. I exert myself
and move the thick-waisted moon
out of her wheeling self-possession

into a gasp in my child's nascent seeing.
I give this tree-caged spirit my remorse
and something of my slyness as I rouse
my art and shelter in the ripples of this pitch.

I am drained of spells and inclination
to command so will only half-bewitch
the seas and watch this biddable spirit
flit new tricks and bend to a tired

and once glorious will when he is
tree-unsheathed by a passing stranger
with a storm-tossed, vacant child as
beloved by him as mine own son by me.

My work is nearly done.
No idle deviltry, no cruelty, no
bloated shows of superior might.
Caliban, attuned

to light and music I can barely sense
will know true freedom by its loss,
wield true power through his subjugation
and trust the moon drunk phases of his birthright.

Quoting Scripture: a Snake Poem
by Wilda Morris

The devil can cite Scripture for his purpose.
An evil soul producing holy witness
Is like a villain with a smiling cheek. . . .
        Antonio in *The Merchant of Venice*

 Study history and see **the** way partisans
associate rivals with the **devil** and themselves
always with the divine. They **can** proclaim the rightness
and justice of their cause. They **cite** Washington,
Jefferson, Lincoln, and even **Scripture** to prove
they are the ones chosen by God **for** leadership.
Do you that believe God chooses **his** (or her) emissaries
on earth according to his **purpose** or how often they quote
verses from the Bible? **An** angry, unforgiving person,
one who is filled with **evil** intent may rail against anyone
who disagrees. *Is his **soul** pure*, I ask,
*if his words are **producing** discord and
hate instead of **holy** love, respect and peace?*
When you **witness** the harvest of the seeds he sows,
ask yourself, **Is** he an example of the devil
speaking, **like** Joseph Goebbels quoting the Sermon on
the Mount, **a** passage put to the purpose of genocide
by a vile **villain** if there ever was one—
a Fascist **with** Hitler's ear, the sidekick to a tyrant,
Goebbels **a** man who used the Christian faith as a weapon,
a **smiling** strategist, killing his compatriots, a man of unholy
cheek. Shakespeare was certainly right.

Prospero & Company Go Way Off Book

by John Sullivan

> Reflections on the Significance of Recently Discovered Rehearsal Notes and "Character Deepening" Routines Developed by Prospero During the Original Production Process for *The Tempest*

Prospero's last ensemble performance – so severely cloistered by geography and limited (at least, among the principals) to "actors" with experiential knowledge of functional sorcery (by practice or, at least, proximity) - has always seemed like much more than just a fashionable Romance written to please James 1st (& entourage), or skeevy Londoner theatre-rabble, or acolytes across time hoping for a change of skin, or even, just sadly cynical us. And stuffing The Tempest into some dramaturgical pigeonhole as yet another symbolic treatise parsing conflicts on the battlefield of humankind's tripartite spiritual nature seems a shame. The fractal dynamic linking Miranda, Caliban and Ariel is pure praxis rooted deep in our souls.

So why, then, were this notes on craft and overarching motivation, along with a pair of devised (then transcribed) performance pretexts consciously forgotten, sealed off in obscure memory-lines, artfully clouded, blurred, obscured forever as ghost-traces, barely sensed: a fleeting aura as the house goes dark. What exactly did Prospero intend to accomplish with his mic-drop performance of *The Tempest*? Surely, something that fundamentally reconfigures the standard holy elements; that still reverberates within the morphology and structure of time-space? Surely, more than a one-off piece of performance art played for a sparse audience of ship-wrecked and deluded co-conspirators. And then, the whole schmear left behind him as a curiously orphaned artifact? And from our vantage in the self-perceived relative future, how do we follow threads of the narrative (extended beyond the Aristotelian parameters of the text), and reassemble the genome of these characters: their actual provenance and pedigrees, various names and aka's, back stories, meandering pathways and convergences, and from the actors perspectives: their true intentions and meta-motivations?

It seems clear that such fragments offer insights and most of our questions would stem from Sycorax, her primary relationship with/to Prospero (are there reasons to believe they were once a hot - but mutually instrumental – item?), and by extension to Caliban: in terms of genetics, progenitor rights ("this thing of darkness I acknowledge mine"), and his role as central symbol of the agonistic dynamic between "civilized" urbanity and wilderness. So many implications radiate from these pivotal-possible connections.

We know the facts given in the text, but: perhaps Sycorax wasn't really dead when Prospero made landfall? And was Miranda, perhaps, yet to be – rather than barely – born. Was Caliban really an orphan? Was Miranda really without a sibling that embodied the eternal epistemic tension between local knowledge, spiritually grounded in place and the necessities of survival, and the elitist prerogatives / rarified expertise of colonial oppression? What did she – or Caliban for that matter - actually embody with two magically inclined parents as possible genetic wild types? (Just saying it.) Was Ariel actually freed or merely trafficked from one owner to another? Was Ariel and her/his ilk part of the presiding *daemon* of this natural space? Was the Island really "empty and undeveloped" (where have we heard that one before?) and, thus, colonized without struggle or (much) bloodshed? Really? And if that transfer of power was contested, who capitulated to whom, and/or what were the terms of the eventual surrender?

And why this convoluted departure from a more or less straighter path toward an aesthetically normalized, tightly scripted production? Probably - though maybe here I betray my own bias toward hermetic excess - to ratchet up the impact of the conjure and rend the veils that compartmentalize time, human intentionality, nature, and geography (both physical and metaphorical). This is not something normally associated with the goals and social purposes of theatre, but Prospero's *Tempest* was, perhaps, to be a real "lever of transcendence," meta-theatrical in the truest sense. Maybe his illusory gale was provoked primarily to hasten the creation of, yet another, "poem of the world," salted with conjunctions, concordances: exposition by analogy and semiotic design, and resonance by way of metaphor and magic.

The excerpts that follow, tagged as <u>Notes</u> and <u>Routines</u>, document this workshop process and offer clues to the riddles in our cascade of why's. The <u>Notes</u> are offered between the <u>Routines</u>, distilling the actor/director's insights and offering advice to the cast. The <u>Notes</u> offer markers, runes and sometimes blatant clues for the actors to help them process and interpret shifts in their feelings, sensations and perceptions – the innermost soul-craft of all forms of acting. However, the <u>Routines</u> seem carefully obscured by foreign (to whom?) languages, speechisms, idiomatic patterns and slang, signs/symbols, semiotic configurations, and social - historical connotations and technologies from past and future destinations. So how does that work?

Most assuredly, Prospero (and possibly Sycorax, as well) traveled through time on "this rough magic" and, of course, brought back with them thickly accreted layers of past and future meanings (much of it deliberately misprised, distorted or misappropriated), and even more layers of site and time specific associations, mannerisms and ideological agendas. Perhaps these alien elements were used to hide the key that might infuse transubstantiating magic into future iterations of *The Tempest*. Then again, since these pieces were never intended for repetition, perhaps there is no actuating key, comprehensible outside Prospero's unique perspective. Considering the play's outcomes (both the overt and the carefully concealed), that conclusion is not inconsistent with the data.

(Director's Note #1)
"So What's the Difference?"

Prospero (to the actors):
Before we leap beyond the normal nets, I'd like you all to open up
To a few observations from a colleague in the faerie troupe of
Oberon & Titania.
Something about the interpenetration of worlds,
Something we've always called theatre magic.
Sometimes it's all dramaturgical;
And sometimes, mostly thaumaturgical.
But in our case, tell me what's the difference?

Where my feet are, that's where it always begins.
Everybody knows that.
But last night my feet drifted and I said
(inside my skin / below my breath):
"O lovely Oberon, please
kiss my ear, please."
So he kissed my ear, and waved dusty light
all around me.
He filled my eyes up with his face.
Or was it the moon?
I can't remember.
I only know my feet swirled air all around.
It eddied like his own breath
against my thighs, pooled around my ankles,
rubbed me blind,
as blind as air it all
began with pure air
and his kiss.
His face.
A moon?
I can't remember.

Prospero (again, to the actors):
All so very meta-meta, no?
But that's how it works, that's how it goes
as you slip into your new skins for our next dance together.
Here's your mantra, croon this tune & morph, baby, morph:

"I know just what I know, I bring it with me, I go inside. Conscious. Then I whisper. Then I'm gone. I learn about it later."
Remember that – forget everything else.
In our case, what's the difference?

Routine 1: (An Interstitial Reading)
"Like Any Witch-Hunt Starts
Where Your Own Feet Are"

(Open on bare stage with ladder. Sycorax climbs down from ladder as 4 track audio background begins: (Track 1) Sycorax nursery tune w / delay-echo w / lisp; (Track 2) muted version of "Trembling" / on Brian Blade's <u>Perceptual</u>; (Track 3) harsh, whispered "Bestir, Viejo … / intro to Part 1; (Track 4) muted sounds of wind and tumult, a ship's mast cracks.)

(Miranda, Caliban and Ariel play approach / avoidance games with masks & hands, taking cues from pieces of the background audio. Sycorax presides center, her staff in both hands above her head like a magic – slightly menacing - *katana*. Audio track stops abruptly.)

(Sycorax raps her staff, two-handed, on the boards with a sharp (possibly amplified) crack. <u>Audio track stops abruptly</u>.) Miranda, Caliban & Ariel stop playing and circle around Sycorax. She adjusts their masks and puts the "kids" to bed. She cradles their heads and smoothes their hair; she pats them and warbles like an old injured bird, throughout.)

(Sycorax climbs back up the ladder to her perch. She breathes loud & slow, carrying her burden of wrack as she climbs. She turns on her perch to address Prospero.)

GO:

Sycorax:
Viejo. Bestir.
Like a soft web in the wind.
Bestir! Bestir!
Like a slow old spider.
Viejo! BESTIR!

(Prospero appears. Sycorax tosses him the staff. She conducts his movements, and the ensuing action with arms & hands.)

(Resume 4 track audio (substitute less-muted version of "Echoes" from Steve Lehman's *Travail, Transformation & Flow* on track 2). Meanwhile, Miranda, Caliban & Ariel sleep the sleep of young spiders.)

(Prospero does *sharkskin-tuxedo shuffle* with his staff. He shuffles circuits around the sleeping spiders and responds to conductive cues from Sycorax: speed change, crouch / extend, twist; he struggles visibly against the twist but moves through this same physical circuit, always "catching" momentarily inside that very twist. As Prospero moves in on the sleeping spiders, they feel his physicality; they try out his movements. They probe and test the air with their legs and arms.)

(After 2-3 circuits by Prospero, Sycorax interrupts.)

Sycorax:
Freeze! Viejo!
(Prospero freezes, mid-twist.)

(Sycorax makes the slow climb down from her perch. She hums her nursery song and makes her own slow circuit: inspecting, adjusting, sniffing and poking "her kids." They respond and continue to spiderize.)

(Sycorax croons her cautionary riff:)

Hush lil' baby don't you cry
Mama gonna' be your big blue eye
And if that big blue eye don't do
Mama gonna' be your brown eye too
And if that brown eye don't get it done
Mama gonna' be your eyeless one
And if that eyeless one ain't true
Mama gonna' sneak
Right up
Go: BOO!

(At BOO! Miranda, Caliban & Ariel activate. They move vigorously, but still experimentally, inside their spider selves.)

(Begin: 3 track version of *Some Last Lines on the Last Page of Prospero's Notorious Book of Practical Dramaturgical Magic* – with separate tracks for Miranda, Caliban & Ariel. Prospero herds them back & forth with the staff.
This conditioning will come in handy later.)

(For rest of action, Sycorax again climbs up onto her perch: The wrack she hauls appears heavier. She reaches the top, holds her head in her palms and alternates labored breathing with sobs.)

(After 1 repetition of audio, Prospero herds "his" spiders off stage by rapping on stage floor with his staff. Audio fades: last natural sound is Sycorax sobbing over soft audio: suggestion – Brian Blades' mellotronic "Down River" from <u>Landmarks</u>.)

Some Last Lines on the Last Page of Prospero's Notorious Book of Practical Dramaturgical Magic

"That the underlying strain of darkness will be overcome or, at least, assimilated."
Paul Zweig

<u>Miranda</u>	<u>Caliban</u>	<u>Ariel</u>
	meanwhile,	
O angel		
Watch	back to the movie:	change
The angel	Tin Town	
Of the city	tan bullet	forever
Is	like we know	
Thee	also	
Raven	real	*por vida*
Watch	almost	
Is also	slow fool	
Terror	sweat	

John Sullivan

Nervous		"when story
What extent	corrido	stops
Dominion		the leak
O angel	total	begins"
Is also	translation	
Thee	of terror	
Vengeance		
Raven	"distant, great	this "strain
Throne	and invisible"	of darkness"
Upon		eaten
Who sits	practice	like air
There	evasion:	"diaphanized"
Dreams		
A format	choose -	don't confuse
For an angel	a	simple
To be	history, or	light
This dream's		with damage
Next dream	you can	
The next	perform	*por vida*
Mouth	it	for good, or
Open		dead, or:
Honor	busted	just sleeping
O angel	seed	inside one
Thee	no room	last
O Horror	no need	free run
Angel	any	dream
Of surge	end	
Nervous	but	murmur-murmur:
Raven	it	my story
Fist		
Of give it		
Up		
Thee-		
O-angel		
Raven	"O acknowledge	
Stare	mine"	every
Mouth open	unexpected	cycle
Wait	true	way
Breathe	as lived before:	short
O angel	it	
Next dream		*por vida*
Also	nexus	
Vengeance	of	foot-

Prospero & Company Go Way Off Book

Nervous
Is Zion
Nervous?
Is
Zion
A lie?
An echo?
Is
Zion
Changed
By
Fear,
By wire,
By locks
Or
Opened
By
Bone
And shine
Into
Next

Into
Next

it, embodies:

a sound,
it
makes

a bed
for
time
to sleep in
a habit of

history
to fly off,
to change
into

next

DONE

prints
run!
run!
change
into
iron
into
water
into skin
up-lift
into
drops
of dazzle

refracts
or mirrors
soft shell
of
a ghost
walks

through
drops
of dreck

(Director's Note #2) "The Last Scene of Prospero's Teatro Begins:"

    baby-fists and baby-toes, a'flailing in the dark,
    shivering and rocking in that amniotic "beauty
    within which all things walk and move": inside a
    dream outside of time, remembered, or not,
    (assembled / unraveled) from residues of memory.

    Lose the mask you wear like a grudge: try
    to remember the first face you can remember.
    Your first face from the last life before it finds (its?) shape.
    Before a stage exists, before any watchers appear, before
    your own map of self and space congeals, (out there / in here), before
    any doors, gates, locks come between your main impulse
    and its most graceful or, at least, more spontaneous expression.
    With every image still latent, on the bare
    edge of the visible.

That face is your full self, it's been said.
    Who else are you then, but your full self,
    it's all been said before.

So begin there: where the body disappears,
and burns (in secret), and impulse
"transluminates" as action. A true and natural
ritual, but sadly, and so often,
diluted and debased.

Routine #2: (The Liminal Piece)
"Through the Portal Where You Go To Catch a Ghost."

Go:

(Sycorax gives Ariel his "skinned head" mask and leads him down/center. Ariel puts skinned head over his own head: like Prospero might fasten a chain around the neck of Caliban.)

(Sycorax adjusts her children – Miranda & Caliban. She adds tension to their accoutrements & their limbs.)

(Prospero removes Sycorax's eyes. 3X he tries to gives her a bowl of light. 3X she refuses to take it. Sycorax stands motionless.)

(Finally, Prospero trades Sycorax his magic staff for a str ong light source that he uses like a ray gun. Prospero walks to the foot of an unfinished crag.)

(Sycorax raps three times on the floorwith staff to begin the *auto-da-fé*. Miranda & Caliban drag Ariel to the foot of the crag.)

(Prospero & Ariel extend crag up & outward using chairs, boxes, various industrial dregs. They fumble in the <u>half-dark</u> as they build. Prospero tries to pull Ariel up the crag: to show him a shiny New Jerusalem. Or some other faerie glamour.)

Prospero:
Up you go. Up you go.

(Prospero hits Ariel full in face with light beam.)

You've been down here too long exposed to the beam. Hurry up.
Time is almost ripe. Time is almost open.
Look. Look up. Now!

Ariel:
OWW!
(Ariel covers his eyes.)
There's too much glare.
I can't get high enough to beat this glare.

(Ariel uncovers his eyes. Ariel puts his hand into the beam & observes himself observing his own hand, etc.)

Look. It all starts inside me. When I look out and see,
Even when I breathe, this glare leaks from inside me, all over the outside.
(Pause.)
This glare starts inside ... of me?

(Prospero pulls Ariel's hands away from the light & hits him full face, again, with the beam. Ariel cups & covers his eyes.)

Propero:
So you'd like to think, but no, you don't remember.
It's all about codes & needs, I tell you, I can read this "Zone of Unlove."
Look up, look out,
Like a camera, not like an eye.

Ariel:
No. I can't beat it ... I won't do it, I ...

(Sycorax picks up the bowl formerly refused and holds it above her head like a chalice. The bowl ignites; becomes, first, a torch, and then a deep well of light.)

(Miranda & Caliban morph into "Mad Max" Doctors / Haz-Mat Handlers / Fellini Clowns. Sycorax leads as eyeless psycho-pomp / cruel concierge. Miranda rides Ariel's back while Caliban goads him with the staff. Sycorax holds the well of light under Ariel's chin & sprinkles a rose trail of funny powders, shards and slivers - the residue of "other peoples' core to die for" - like the sower and her seed,
or the con and her mark.)

(Ariel snuffles, snorts, sneezes, strains to resist this trail's gravity, but always feels the inevitable pull, the drag of destiny, or personal inertia. And so, always returns to the work. Always seeking the true event horizon: the real gist of Messiaen's *Quartet for the End of Time*.)

(A bass line comps this "Dance of the Doctors." The line is muffled like a stereo inside a closed car. A thump more felt than heard.)

(Prospero holds the strong beam focus mostly on his own face while he talks to Ariel. Sometimes, he lights up the Doctors and their dance. Sometimes, he shines the light into "this Zone, this Ocean." For punctuation. To keep the audience up on its toes, or back on its heels. Then he shines it full onto his own face.)

Prospero:
(Begins tracking "Dance of the Doctors" with his beam. This conversation between Prospero and Ariel is both prior and ongoing.)

... Hah! So you think. But now: Be. Hold.
It's a world. Just a world. Maybe, it's a live one.
Maybe it's a shiny, bomber, snarl, strobe,
freakin' needle all-a-time tickin'
like a clever Bauhaus watch.

It's a world: but maybe it's a big red nose ...
Maybe it's that damn / mad / uncanny Bauhaus umbrella steady
doggin' all your dreams.
Hey, maybe it's that spooky face in your rear view mirror -
The one that bobs into focus: slow, like one-frame-a-second up,
And down, and gone. Hah! Done and gone.
Hah! So far down and still too gone to pin.
Like some kinda' science.
Hah! This "bright moment" cannot be caught, cannot be bought.
Cannot be served like a stretch.
Or some kinda' séance.
(Pause.)
It's a damn world, that's right. It's a straight world's
Sop to ... this ... old ... heart, me boy-O.
One full eyeful of gall and bane. One sick cuppa' hootch. With a
raw edge. With no bottom. With a bad sick glow. Leaves a rattle
in your throat, now, don't it?
(Pause.)
Hey, somebody, hella' tell me: if the deal down here
is so damn crazy,
Then why is the air between us so so-very-sad?
(Pause.)
Brother? Color? Trade one eye for another?
There's no more dream of heaven left.
So where-did-it-go?
(Pause.)
And what are we gonna' feed our angel when there's
no more dream of heaven left?
No more. No where. Not-no-never one eye for another.
(Pause.)
Tell you what, long time this angel's got to live blind,
on air alone. Bright air. Diaphanized.
Blood-steam shower of grace; Bite down!
Real steel dagger on the tip of heaven's tooth:
You, best bite down on it.
(Ariel interrupts.)

Ariel:
Hey! You gotta' stop this, old man.
It ain't about us now. It's them.
Them against them, now.

Prospero & Company Go Way Off Book

(The Dance of the Doctors turns back toward the crag. At " ... one big eye floats on the cold skin of this ocean ..." the Doctors dump Ariel back
at the foot of the crag and park there..)

Prospero:
Them, them, them ... Hah!

(Prospero hits Ariel full in face with light beam.)

Gotcha!
You a wound, or a mouth, or a fool, or what?
All-a-time you say them ... them,
And I say listen: now. OOOOO!   Feel it like a wet feather.
Like a world's slow seep of shadow into blood, into bone.
Cold lung, cold sea, cold needle bass go reverb
And my brain says: suck it up, baby.
Like: a-boom-ba-boom-boom, ba-ba-boom-boom & etc.
Unto you. Joy Channel.
Til the big engine turns its beam.
Unto you. Watching you.
And You. Unto It.
Just You. Watching back.
(Pause.)
You salt, you sad air, fog every morning in a lie, alone.
It ain't no accident. And it's got no payoff.
(Pause & Gather.)
Don't let it. Dislodge. Spin away fast. Down and gone.
It's got no payoff. It's no damn accident.
(Pause: to Sigh Away the Walkin' Blues.)
So you gotta' wish. So you gotta' wish. So you gotta' wish.
(Pause: to Preach the Right Words / to Charm Open All the Locks.)
Somewhere. You gotta' wish. Then you gotta' wish. More.
Now, you gotta' look up. Somewhere. So you gotta' wish. Again.
And you wish, and you wish, and you wish. Somewhere. Then:
you for real see IT: This Zone. This Ocean.
(Pause: to Unclench & Just Breathe.)

Now, somewhere. One big eye floats
on the cold skin of this Ocean.
(Longer than normal 3-4 beat Pause.)
Brother. Color.   Sweet angel, long time exposed to the beam. One eye down. One eye gone. So you gotta' wish, so you gotta' ... wish. And time is, and time was and, now, time's almost ripe. Time's almost open. Just Now ...just right now. No great dream of heaven. Now. Just this gotta' wish. Just This. Gotta' wish. Just This...This...Ocean.

DONE

Even Shakespeare Knew, a Mesostic Poem
by Wilda Morris

Who will believe thee, Isabel? ~ Angelo in *Measure for Measure*, by William Shakespeare

        It is the fate of **W**oman
                t**H**at few blame a man
        if **O**ne seduces her.

            When her belly expands
    even due to rape, **I**t's true—
some say she tempted the **L**out
                unti**L** he gave in.

    She may report him, **B**ut may
          want to hid**E**
              from ug**L**y words,
    protect her reputat**I**on
   from attack by thos**E** who always
           say how a**V**idly a woman
           will chas**E**

            and **T**ry her Adam. A woman
           w**H**o
        aspir**E**s to do good
         Each day, and

           l**I**ve contentedly.
    What then **S**hould she do?
       Wh**A**t would you do—
   turn your **B**ack,
      on h**E**r
         or **L**isten and give her justice?

A Bard in the Forest of Arden
by Kate Falvey

So where are all the fools and fairies?
Quince, you string the lights and rig the gauzy scrim.
Titania, shimmer all your sylvan innuendo in
and vary like an otherworldly whim or
a thought before the sin.

Rustics, do some heavy lifting
within that copse of wizened, watching oak.
Improvise some slapstick and rough jokes,
collide with fairy folk and shadow Peter Quince.
A little bumbling heedlessness will not go amiss.

Puck, you flit like madness in the wind
tickling through the audience as they queue.
You won't have much to do before we start the show.
Just stir the moonlight into drowsy possibility
and slink through boughs like spectral glow.
Don't be too lascivious and listen for your cue.

Lovers, try not to seem blasé when you collect the cash,
even with our quasi-futuristic theme.
We aim for authenticity with our mash-up and re-scripting --
a reverential homage to the dream. Let your bawdy be a bit
Elizabethan as you grope. It's ok to poke some weary
through the naughty as you dodge, emote, and flit.

The moon swells with silver serendipity,
a scallop shell of opalescent breath,
whispering of weird verges and spilling ghostly webs
into our semi-woodsy set. There are still birches left
and their silver peelings glimmer in the dark.
And there is that ancient oak, old when first he dreamed
and then he wrote.

Now, sprites, the music! Time to pluck
the stems of eglantine and oxlip
to wind around the infant prince.

This old wreck of a wood will fill out nicely
and convince the rabble with our borrowed, re-worked,
slightly campy, but ever-faithful twists.

Douse this scraggly wood with mystical pretend
and England become Athens once again.

Dear Helena,
by Elizabeth Sylvia

> *I am your spaniel – A Midsummer Night's Dream*

When you told Demetrius
that the girl he lusted for

was headed for the forest
with the boy she wanted in her turn

and then you followed him
with hopes that he

would beat you like his dog,
I knew you were someone I could talk to.

Say want is a shadow twin
beguiling all our deeds, a double

with us in the sac, a night-comforter
and eater from our plate. Don't let

me deny want is my sister. Help
me own her
          For I can
take little from love's platter

though offered. I make love
like the messenger bee,

treasuring the glinting dust
the flower shakes away.

Helena, you do not want these ways.
Your want is grasping, adores the face

of its shame, feels hot in the cold,
does not care if in the end

you lick stolen love dropped
by Oberon off the back of a truck.

Teach me to want so.
That I should not even need

a potion to admit how I have
longed for an ass's head.

Antonio's Waves: (A meditation on Twelfth Night)

by Nicholas Yandell

When I look to the waves,
I see an origin story.
A moment of tension,
Unresolved,
Refusing to cease.

My introduction,
His desperate bobbing form,
Scarcely differentiated from the surrounding flotsam.
Slick skin as I pulled him to the boat,
Air reentering his body,
His vitality surging suddenly through me.

When one saves a protagonist,
They are typically framed as a hero,
But not me.
I'm left pining.
After a destined necessity,
In a famous playwright's story,
Which also includes me,
As the character who usually gets forgotten.

I've dedicated my life to the sea.
Grappling rope with calloused hands,
Guiding vessels through the swells,
Grown comfortable in their deadly power.

Enduring these trials unflinchingly,
Until that drifted offering,
An unknown beast,
Whose tail I grasped,
Dragging me through the pages,
Of a future more near to death,
Than any hazardous voyage.

The plot moved on,
Through a dozen nights,
Of purposeful facades and mistaken identities,
Disparate fragments,
Chaotically finding completion,
Except for me...

This story was never mine.

I still exist of course,
Heartbroken,
Because I don't easily move on.
Not so fluid and adapting,
Like my rippling companions,
I am the rocks jutting out,
As they crash around me.

Despite where I am,
I don't regret submerging the unknown waters.
The brief spell that was born.
The passion that surfaced the salty storm,
Dissolving the steady life I've known.

Even the rejection,
Dispersing the spell,
Awakened in me,
New possibilities.

Left alone by the Master's pen,
Drifting buoyantly,
Not weighed down by the closure,
Of couplings or tragedies or comic happenings.

Life isn't always about the longer narrative.
The short passages can be the most poignant of all.
Those dangling with no resolve,
Left only completed through dreams, imagination, or acceptance.

My story may always be,

Just a sordid introduction to an inner self,
Forcefully suppressed,
But powerful enough to break through,
Splashing out of the words on the pages,
And floating freely,
To surge with the swells,
Of new beginnings.

Bottom
by Frank De Canio

Peaseblossom, Cobweb, Mustardseed
and Moth all will attend his need,
Titania deems in Shakespeare's "Dream".
Midsummer Night's subversive scheme
permits this Fairy to reverse
the roles, so groom now bears the purse.
And though it may appear a boon
to be a 'tended to' buffoon,
when sprites become your fancy's guides,
because the Queen of Fairies chides
them to be at your beck and call,
are you a reigning lord or thrall?
And since a sprite's not gender-bound,
how can a Bottom stand his ground?

TRAGEDIES

Vengeance is in my heart, death in my hand, Blood and revenge are hammering in my head.

Titus Andronicus, Act 2, Scene 3

shakespeare zombie
by RC deWinter

when you're afraid to live and afraid to die
every day is a conundrum

to be
or
not to be

the question calcifies your soul

living involves risk failure heartache pain
fear sits in your stomach like a rock
as you grind your teeth and bite your nails

not living slaps you in the face with a
great blank wall beyond which is
heaven or hell or nothing at all

so you tiptoe through the day
as best you can while the rock shifts
gnawing your innards with every step

at night the rock rises to your throat
as you fight sleep because
who knows if you'll see another sunrise

it's no way to be and yet you don't want
not to be

caught in a halfworld of shadows
you're the walking dead
a cardboard corpse

going through the motions

Weird Sisters
by Elizabeth Sylvia

Where hast thou been, sister? –Macbeth

Since the night I was born I've
known howling at the moon, mixed
yours with my own, crossed all times rhymes
together by the born beards
on our faces. Even when apart
women's tales never tell
& so sisterhood snakes up
the world of men, saying good
riddance
to each girl pulled
from the tree like a pulpy
plum, maybe mouthful of sour
for the biter. Weird sisters pick
our own women, don't you know
by the way our sunken bodies
suck up all the light, small as a nutshell
big as the moor, tying time in a bow,
not beautiful for any price but
driving men mad exposing all the hidden
swords they make of words.

I'll
kiss
to
your beard
of hurt
and call
us
lords
of this
world
ugly
absurd
wicked
I've no
ready
spell
to know
what
woman
is.

A Carving
by James B. Nicola

Uncouth it was, a fall from grace,
but when we passed the thick-barked tree
I heard it, rustling, asking me

to carve initials on its face—
four—enclose them, and then trace
a heart around them, making two
one, albeit metaphorically.

For Antony and Romeo
are known only from what was later
written of them; but we know

Abelard from what he penned
himself! You see, I couldn't wait. Or
maybe I didn't care who'd see,
nor how the hell the tale might end,

but could no longer bear to be
but half a whole, with-out the heart
wherein I blaze as one with you.

Iago Resides Inside the Insane Asylum
by John Davis

Every liar loves a laugh. Got to love the grief
    a handkerchief can bring. As sharp as a reef

that handkerchief, my bully beef, a gold leaf for a
    sneak thief. What a relief at last to be lieutenant

not that wax plant Cassio. About as brave as
    an eggplant. Probably pees his pants. Trust—

what a bust that is. I'd rather lust, slide
    a corsage on Desdemona's bust, do some office

twixt her sheets. Othello, you jealous fellow,
    if you won't be my lover, then go smother

your wife with a pillow. Any wife of mine won't
    shine. She'll wither on the vine if she declines

to hide my secret. It's nothing a knife can't decide.
    Swift slice. Talk about deadline. So nice this life

living on the fault line. Kill here. Kill there.
    I'm the heir of revenge. Who can't I upend

and suspend from breath. Jealousy, my green-eyed
    monster friend, whose meat shall we feed on today?

A POUND OF FLESH
by Roy Schreiber

Cast
Jessica - Woman in her early twenties
Shylock - Man in his late fifties to early sixties

Scene: *A room in Shylock's house in 16th century Venice. Shylock sits at a table stacked with coins. He dresses in a long black robe that has yellow wheel patches on the shoulder and a larger one on his chest. He sits at a table, counts the coins and records them in a notebook, writing with a black quill. A barrette style yellow hat lies on the far corner of the table. Jessica appears in the doorway and walks in. She is elegantly dressed and wears a necklace with a cross at the end.*

JESSICA
I'm surprised you agreed to see me.

SHYLOCK
I'm surprised you asked to come back after you abandoned me. Stole from me.

JESSICA
I know you'll find it hard to believe, but what happens to my father does matter to me.

SHYLOCK
Would you be surprised if I said I thought you had a strange way of showing it.

JESSICA
Jews and Christians both have a commandment to honor their father. I honor you.

SHYLOCK
You honor me by running off with a Christian and taking everything of value in the house you could carry.

JESSICA
What I did had nothing to do with how I felt about you.

SHYLOCK
Even if I had chosen to ignore what you did, we Jews are a small community here. What you do reflects on me.

JESSICA
I cannot live my life as though we inhabit the same body.

SHYLOCK
Jews have other ways of expressing their discontent that do not involve stealing. And marrying Christians.

JESSICA
I married for love. Not to prove any point.

SHYLOCK
Even though you marry that Christian...

JESSICA
Lorenzo.

SHYLOCK
Lorenzo. I still have hope for you.

JESSICA
That is not what I've heard. I've heard you consider me dead.

SHYLOCK
If you heard I went to the synagogue and had the rabbi declare you dead, you heard a lie.

JESSICA
Of the various things I thought you might do, that was never one of them.

SHYLOCK
Why?

JESSICA
Since mother died, I can't remember you inside the synagogue. If you went in now to the rabbi about me, he would ask you to

pay for the declaration.

SHYLOCK
He has already declared enough of my children dead. My Leah, too.

JESSICA
Perhaps if I had been a boy, things would have been different between us.

SHYLOCK
I gave you all the freedoms you could ever want. Just like a boy. God's reward for this good deed? You met the Christian and became his wife.

JESSICA
If you had tried to lock me up, you were wise enough to know I would have escaped. But I must confess. I'm glad for your wisdom.

SHYLOCK
Enough of your flattery. Why have you come?

JESSICA
To offer you a proposal.

SHYLOCK
A term that implies money.

JESSICA
A proposal that involves money, among other things.

SHYLOCK
I'm listening.

JESSICA
I offer to give back mother's turquoise ring in return for a favor, one that will insure you a handsome profit as well.

SHYLOCK
You begin your proposal by offering me Leah's first gift to me, something that is already mine in return for a favor.

JESSICA
Here I play by your rules. You would say possession matters.

SHYLOCK
What is the favor?

JESSICA
Take the money Bassanio offers.

SHYLOCK
No.

JESSICA
You refuse his money in repayment of Antonio's loan from you?

SHYLOCK
I will demand the alternative.

JESSICA
The pound of flesh.

SHYLOCK
A pound of flesh.

JESSICA
Flesh over money. I thought I knew you.

SHYLOCK
Do you know anything about Venetian law?

JESSICA
Why do you ask?

SHYLOCK
Because once you marry, all your worldly goods belong to your husband, not you. Before you married, they were mine.

JESSICA
Lorenzo agreed to let me use the ring in my proposal.

SHYLOCK
I presume he has a motive.

JESSICA
Bassanio and Antonio are his friends. Now, mine too.

SHYLOCK
So, of all the things you took, the two of you offer to return me Leah's ring.

JESSICA
I know you treasure it.

SHYLOCK
And now you want to dangle the prospect of its return before me to get what you want.

JESSICA
As a young girl, I could never find a way to tell you what mattered to me. Now, perhaps, I have.

SHYLOCK
And you think playing the role of a bargaining thief will make up for all you've taken from me?

JESSICA
If you had arranged a Jewish match for me, how much would my dowry have cost you? My guess is even more than I have given Lorenzo.

SHYLOCK
When that so-called dowry is gone, do you really think this Christian will stay with you?

JESSICA
I am now a Christian. We married in a Christian church where marriage is a sacrament and lasts as long as we two shall live.

SHYLOCK
Your mother was a Jew. Therefore you are a Jew. You will always be a Jew. All the laws, Jewish, Christian, and Venetian, forbid Christians and Jews to marry.

JESSICA
You talk as if being born a Jew was the same as being born a black-a-moor.

SHYLOCK
Do you remember what happened when that black-a-moor general married a young Venetian noble woman?

JESSICA
Her father approved the match.

SHYLOCK
The black-a-moor strangled her.

JESSICA
A self-professed villain masquerading as his friend took advantage of him.

SHYLOCK
What kind of friends does your husband have?

JESSICA
Friends who wish him well.

SHYLOCK
And who among them wishes you well? A bankrupt forced to marry for money. A man who spits on me.

JESSICA
Friends who look for ways to bring joy and song into both our lives whenever they can.

SHYLOCK
Sing all the masses with them you want. Dance with them in a public square. You'll always be a Jew. To these friends of his and to the rest of the world. And to me.

JESSICA
You've raised all of this to distract from the bargain I offer you.

SHYLOCK
No. I raise all of this in the hope I can awaken you from what you think is your dream. It's really your nightmare.

JESSICA
With your demand for a pound of flesh, you will turn every-

thing into a nightmare for everyone. Even you.

SHYLOCK
Why do you defend this merchant, Antonio?

JESSICA
For your sake as much as his.

SHYLOCK
His sake, as you put it, is what matters to me now.

JESSICA
He comes before your own interests?

SHYLOCK
This man has loathed and disrespected me from the moment we laid eyes on each other.

JESSICA
He's your rival in business. You often get the better of him. Venetian merchants do not take such matters as if they were Greek philosophers.

SHYLOCK
If, as they say, business is business, I would have no complaint with him. But he always took his behavior toward me further than that. As he said himself, because I am a Jew.

JESSICA
He wanted to get under your skin, tempt you to do foolish things that would give him the advantage. If you go ahead with this trial, he will have what he wants.

SHYLOCK
No. He's miscalculated. I will get under his skin.

JESSICA
Your reasoning mystifies me. Bassanio, the man who needed the money in the first place, has offered to pay you double the original loan. He now has a rich, clever wife and can well afford to pay. Why refuse him?

SHYLOCK
For me, Bassanio has nothing to do with this.

JESSICA
I thought profit from trade gave you genuine pleasure. How much more profitable than double can you expect?

SHYLOCK
Profit comes in many forms.

JESSICA
How is a pound of flesh profit?

SHYLOCK
I take it from a man who has kicked me, spit on me, has spoken evil and untrue things about me to anyone who will listen. Do you think others with whom I trade and seek profit will respect me if I behave like a Christian and turn the other cheek?

JESSICA
Surely everyone will respect a profit of double the original loan.

SHYLOCK
No, they won't.

JESSICA
You seem very certain.

SHYLOCK
The world will call Antonio sly. Admire him. Say he makes another man feel guilty and pay off a loan that not legally his. Antonio would gain credit for paying nothing. I would gain no credit.

JESSICA
But you would lose none.

SHYLOCK
I need the Christians to fear and respect me or they will behave like Antonio. I will have my pound of flesh from him.

JESSICA
You seem terribly confident that a Christian court will uphold a

Jew.

SHYLOCK
I grant you, here in Venice, they make Jews wear yellow hats and badges. They even lock us in our houses at night.

JESSICA
You ignore their prejudices at your peril.

SHYLOCK
It's all for show in the Christian world. In the end, they need us. As long they feel guilty about charging interest to one another, they need us. They need me.

JESSICA
I don't see how that helps you in court.

SHYLOCK
The laws of Venice governing trade are for all, Christians and Jews. What if other Jews saw me treated unjustly? What then for the Venetians who need to borrow from them? From me?

JESSICA
But what if you're wrong? What if the court finds a way to rule against you and still give the appearance of handing out justice?

SHYLOCK
We are no fools. They cannot play games with us and expect us to shrug our shoulders and go on as if they treated us fairly.

JESSICA
They are no fools either. Don't underrate them. All it takes is one person to find a weakness in your case, and you are out your money. And your revenge.

SHYLOCK
No. I will get my pound of flesh and the respect and their fear that will come with it.

The End

To My Last Syllable
by Debbie Peters

After William Shakespeare's
  "The Tragedy of Macbeth" (Act 5, Scene 5, lines 17–28)

His hour upon the stage
Was a tale well told
Full of love and meaning
Signifying everything.

Time should stop
When one so special no longer is.
The sun should not rise
Nor the moon shine.

But life's walking shadow
Creeps on in its petty pace
And I am left with no one
Who has lived in my skin.

I am heard no more.
I will strut and fret
In the fury of grief's void
To my last syllable.

Ophelia
by Ed Higgins

Her ghost
kept coming back
to Hamlet
maybe driving him
mad as well who knows

trailed by pale regret
and her sad specter
(haunted undersea dreams
of the innocent drowned)

his mist-thin love
incapable of saving her
but oh, her fair fey hair
glistening, floating there

lost love's shudder rising
over Elsinore's
blood-hazed moon.

Death's deep chill
moaning loudly
this ghostly loss too.

Denmark's knowing
defects of weather--
winds blowing cold
north-by-northwest

warning of darker skies
coming still.

Ode to Cordelia
by Shakti Pada Mukhopadhyay

Who loved best?
Was she Goneril, Regan or Cordelia?
Oh Cordelia! Your unspoken love
Lear couldn't feel.
You didn't flatter your father,
but fought your wicked sisters
to win back your father's land.
You refused to color your feelings,
as you were honest and virtuous,
unlike your greedy and cruel sisters.
You were stubborn and proud,
but your greatness wished
if love could replace evil and greed.

When fortune had frowned upon Lear,
he sought your forgiveness.
He prayed to sing like birds in the cage
with you and to tell the old tales.
When he had come out with your dead body
in his arms, he praised your voice as soft,
gentle and low, like the shining qualities of a woman.
Not a small place this world is,
to feel your sacrifice for all the injustice
and evils done upon you.

Sonnet At Last
by Teresa Sari FitzPatrick

Ever since the birth of Ophelia
Those of us who sing aloud
For no reason have garnered
Strange looks from the silent

But when the angel falls
When the phoenix burns
When the birth cry finally comes
Lips have no recourse but parting

After comes the quiet death
The ash, the flowers, the blood and yet
The still orgastic seed of spring
Forever breaks its moldering husk
Bursting out and tearing off
And ripping me apart again.

A Short Summary of the Aubade from Romeo and Juliet Act 3, Scene 5
by David de Young

JULIET: Nightingale.
ROMEO: Lark.
JULIET: Meteor.
ROMEO: Come, death, and welcome! Juliet wills it so.
JULIET: Lark.
ROMEO: Oh, fuck!
Enter NURSE.

Parsing #3
by Karla Linn Merrifield

Oh, noblest of efforts by novices
this spring evening not gone unnoticed.

Such potent nouns summoned to play at names—
monotony, tears, regret— & verb games:

present tense, past tense, return present tense—
with echoes of Romeo's dawning sense;

with *deep down inside, inside my heart*
doubling the mind's pain at lost love's new start.

And *nothing improved, nothing good remained.*
The passive voice? This poem by it gained.

A Shakespearean curse
by Timothy Arliss OBrien

The fae I found blessed me one winter day
The way the act of how to give a curse
Be swift with me and I will have my say
Be wary before I rise and spill this verse.

I bless you here with this Shakespearean curse:
(A perfect Shakespearean sonnet)

May all your words fall in iambic foot.
May star-crossed lovers miss each other oft.
And when you grasp for stars they turn to soot.
For once you catch your dreams they leave aloft.

Your comedies from tragedies arise
And fail the potions that you try to brew
And lovers leave you for the bigger skies
All witches and the fae be against you.

The priests and gods shall be of no more help
And things will never be as they are seen.
For malice shall be every card you're dealt.
And everyone you see shall be a fiend.

So mote it be this harmless little curse
Begone, beware, before you're in a hearse.

Weirds to Stage
by Anna Laura Falvey

We set ourselves
out at dawn when there's nothing
but brinesoak'd air and heath.

The least weird of our sisters takes
out a green Crayola marker and colored
in a burnt orange leaf this morning. The ink
was too thin: too much water, not enough pigment,
running black between the veins.

The weirdest of our sisters clutches
a stick in vicegrip. Teeth sharp as grimalkin,
they sink their incisors into the softwood
and slack their jaw, the branch their new
upper lip, top of the face.

The most neutral weird of our sisters rips
clumps of heather by the purple root,
threading thin, hairlike stems through
the cracks in their fingernails, counting
as they go. By high noon, there is a tapestry.

We stage ourselves, set
out at dawn to wait, when there's nothing
but brinesoak'd air and heath.

Save for the chopped saltjaw wind
which whips soft clothes to skin,
notathing separates our bodies

from the moorland's breath
as we wait for the scene to begin.

Mercutio's Lament
by Valerie Hunter

Romeo, I thought I knew you.
You were a sap for pretty girls
(or any girl, really),
a little melodramatic, but sharp-witted,
and also my best friend,
the only one who always understood my puns,
who always understood *me*.

When you refused to fight,
I thought I understood;
Tybalt's a master swordsman, and you,
well, you're a lovesick fool.
I took your place
because that's what best friends do.
I could hold my own,
Tybalt wasn't mad at me.

But you forgot the rules somewhere,
you couldn't leave well enough alone.
Never mind why you came between us,
never mind that I was hurt under your arm.
That hurt is just a scratch
compared to the desperation in your eyes,
desperation that I know has nothing
to do with me or my imminent death.

You have a secret,
something so pure and good
that it radiates from you like starlight,
makes you look like some angel of the heavens.
Maybe that sight should give me comfort,
here in my final moments,
but it doesn't.

I curse you,
your family,
your damned feud,

but really all I want to ask
is why you held this secret close,
kept it from me, your best friend,
the one who gave his life for you.

Romeo, I thought I knew you,
but I was dead wrong,
and now just dead.

Shakespeare Did Not Know How My Mother Would Die: a Trimeric Poem

by Wilda Morris

Cowards die many times before their deaths;
The valiant never taste of death but once.
Of all the wonders that I yet have heard.
It seems to me most strange that men should fear.

The valiant never taste of death but once,
Shakespeare wrote, but he was wrong,
It's not just cowards with more deaths than one.

Of all the wonders that I yet have heard,
most awful was the day my mother said
she no longer knew the name she gave me.

It seems to me most strange that men should fear
to die of accident or heart attack. Much worse,
it seems to me, to die as Mother did, piece by piece.

NOTE: The first four lines are from *Julius Caesar* by William Shakespeare.

SHAKESPEARE'S GHOST
by Kathryn Paulsen

Ghosts walk, and there are witnesses.
Dead men live to tell their tales.
We, to hear and wonder, keep the watch,
and dream of vengeance, execute the play.

Let love go, she will not stay thee
from thy god-invited way. Death calls
for death. A little company is all
that makes release from this life bearable.

Murmurs 'round night-fires, tossing off stars,
caress of moon-breast under her clouds, a fair
eclipse or comet to enjoy, coy lips of lightning—
whispering words thou'st never heard alive.

Yet still you live among us,
along with him who made you
who hears the sighs, the cries, the cheers
of crowd after crowd after crowd
on night after night after night,
  dreaming forever,
in his tempest-tossed seas.

Ophelia Laughs
by Kate Falvey

as the crow-flowers tickle and the nettles prick
her remembrances.
she is a river of dream purpling the shadows
of overhanging branches as,
mermaid-like a while, she buoys herself up
with flow and flight,
no more the awkward baggage of a boy
with clanking ghostly chains for brains.

Night is Over and Day is Almost Here
by Z.B. Wagman

"What's wrong now?" The exasperation in Thea's voice echoed around the auditorium. As soon as her words broke through the scene, the two actors in front of her retreated to opposite corners of the stage like boxers who had just heard the bell. Thea couldn't help but sigh as she approached the stage, sliding up onto it with practiced ease.

Things were not going well. It was the night before the show opened and they were still struggling through the basics. It was her own fault, Thea knew. It had been her decisions that had led them here. It was her inexperience which had lost them their star actor less than a week before opening night. It was her fault for thinking that she could even direct a show in the first place. But now she had no choice but to push through.

"What's going on?" she asked as she got to her feet. Though both actors stood three feet above her onstage, neither of them could meet her eye. "Why wasn't that working?"

"Don't look at me," the woman muttered. Her acrid tone did more than merely shift the blame. She crossed her arms and finally met Thea's gaze. "I've been ready to perform for months." Rosalind was the local prima donna and Thea's leading lady. She starred in every show that the Arden Community Theater had put on over the last ten years and had an ego that matched. Well into her thirties, Rosalind was the very picture of beauty: her flame red hair and alabaster skin gave off the impression of having a delicate, paper thin exterior, while her hard eyes and sarcastic wit let everyone know that she had a heart of steel. All this prowess was being aimed at the boy standing across the stage from her.

In comparison, Trayvon Rogers looked like a baby. Barely sixteen, he seemed to stumble through life without the confidence that comes naturally to boys of his age. He wilted under Rosalind's gaze and Thea couldn't help but be reminded that he was not her first choice. "I just don't understand what's going on here," Trayvon said and Thea could tell that he was trying to keep the whine out of his voice.

"It's romance," Rosalind said with a scoff. "Some of the greatest ever written."

"I get that. I do!" he said in response to Rosalind's eye roll. "I'm just a little confused at what's actually happening. All these wilt thous and therefores, it's like it's not even written in english."

Thea cut off Rosalind's groan with a wave of her hand. "Okay, let's go through it again. Don't worry about the lines this time. Just say whatever you think they mean."

Trayvon nodded though a worried grimace cut across his face as he made his way to the giant bed in the center of the stage. Rosalind shot Thea a pointed look.

"Just play along," the director sighed. They had gone over all of this with their original star. Mike had had little trouble understanding Shakespeare's prose, but Thea had insisted on spending a couple of weeks seated at a table talking through line by line translations. All that time wasted…If she had known, there would have been so many other things she could have done with that time.

As the two actors slipped beneath the sheets, Thea returned to her seat in the audience. As she sank into the cushions, she turned to the only other person in the room. "Glaurea, can you watch the script and make sure they don't stray too far."

The dumpy woman beside Thea pushed up her glasses and leaned closer to the binder that sat on a card table in front of her. Glaurea was the stage manager, which meant that it was her job to make sure that Thea could focus on the actors instead of worrying about any of the millions of things that happened behind the scenes. She gave Thea an officious nod and the director turned back to the stage.

"Alright, remember: you've just had your first night together. It was better than anything you could have imagined."

"Hold on," Rosalind said with mock seriousness. "That's something some of us can *only* imagine."

"Hey!" Trayvon replied, his cheeks darkening in a blush.

Thea cut off the rest of his retort. "Focus. Come morning, you both know that Romeo has to leave. If anyone finds him here they will kill him."

Trayvon nodded solemnly from his side of the bed but Rosalind's eyes only reflected her amusement.

"Okay, get ready. You can start whenever you feel like it."

With one last smirk from Rosalind, the couple closed their eyes. They lay silent for a few seconds in a striking tableau. Limbs entangled, Trayvon's dark skin cut a stark contrast to Rosalind's light. It was an image that Thea wished she had planned.

Gently Trayvon shook his head and sat up. As he yawned and stretched Rosalind stirred as well. "Do you have to go? It can't be day yet. Ignore the birds, they're only nightingales. Every night they sing on the tree underneath my window. Come back to bed." Even though this was a simple walkthrough, it seemed as if the sarcastic Rosalind from moments earlier was gone. In her place was the gentle Juliet, staring at Trayvon with eyes that could only be those of a love-sick teenager.

Trayvon, for his part, looked only marginally more confident than before. "It was a lark no nightingale. Look love, what…beautiful colors the clouds are in the east?" He glanced imploringly towards Thea who sighed to herself yet again, but to her actor she just nodded encouragement. It was close enough. "Night is over and the day is almost here. I must either live and leave, or stay and die."

"That's not daylight it's…a meteor! It'll guide you on your journey tonight. So stay, it's not time to leave." The mask of Juliet slipped a little bit from Rosalind's face as she played up the absurdity of what she was saying. Rarely did Rosalind smile, and it was nice for Thea to see that this process hadn't crushed her sense of humor.

Trayvon embraced the dramatics that Rosalind had tapped into. "Let me be taken and put to death," the boy rolled up onto his knees, hands raised in supplication as he begged with Rosalind. "I'm happy if you are! If you think the sunrise is just a trick of the light or the bird is no lark; I have more care to stay than will to go: come death and welcome! Juliet wills it so."

Thea wondered if he had slipped back into verse on purpose. But that worried her less than the fact that everything from the smile stretched across his face to the trembling of his hands spoke of the neuroses of a teenaged boy. Nowhere on that stage did she see an inkling of the suave, romantic Romeo; he was Trayvon through and through.

Silence stretched on onstage and both actors turned towards each other with looks that plainly said, "your turn."

Glaurea's stern voice floated out of the darkness. "You've got a little bit more Trayvon: 'How is't, my soul? Let's talk: it is not day.'"

"Shit," Trayvon said softly, his smile evaporating. "Uh, how are you? Tell me because it's not day."

Rosalind rolled her eyes but when she saw the mortified look on Trayvon's face she smiled, "It is, it is: now get the fuck outa here. It's a lark that ruins everything. Like totally just destroys every. Single. Thing. Fuck larks. Now leave. It's getting lighter with every second you waste."

A weak smile reappeared on Trayvon's lips as he finished the scene, "More light and light: more dark and dark our woes!"

For a second the actors stared into each other's eyes. "Good enough," Thea said and they broke away from each other, once again retreating to opposite ends of the stage. "Did that make sense to you?"

Trayvon nodded, "Thanks for letting me do that." Though he was looking at Thea, she had the distinct impression that he was speaking to Rosalind.

"Very good, both of you," Thea swept her gaze over to include Rosalind. The woman gave her a wry smile in response. "Let's take five and come back to this later."

#

Later that night, after both actors had left, Thea and Glaurea sat in the silent auditorium pouring over their notes. "There's one thing I keep coming back to," Thea said, pawing through the papers in front of her. She sat in the very center of the stage, notebook pages and sketches spread out all around her. On her lap was a stack of papers well worn with highlights and scribbles—her script. It had been creased and torn, half of it was missing, and someone had decided to doodle cats all over the front page. Thea now sat trying to read the words behind the doodles. "Why did I ever decide to do this? Theater takes so much effing work."

Glaurea just grunted in response. Unlike the director, she had been a part of productions at the Arden Community Theater for more than a decade now. While each of those shows had brought their own unique challenges, a common theme between them all was the incessant bemoaning of the creative staff. While actors and directors complained about how their costumes didn't fit right or wished that the set could be built faster, it was Glaurea's job to oversee that everything came together in time for the show. Where the creatives saw their production as a priceless gem—something so unique that it could never be replicated—Glaurea just saw another battle of efficiency.

Glaurea sat in the first row of the audience, the card table in front of her neatly stacked with piles of papers. As she peered down at her script she absentmindedly tucked back a wisp of her thick black hair that had escaped the cage of her ponytail. She was typing up the line notes from that night's run-through and there were a lot of them.

"I don't know if we're going to make it," Thea said to the room at large before laying back in the middle of the floor.

Night is Over and Day is Almost Here

Glaurea ignored her. In her experience, every director felt this way the night before the first show…though in this case it might just be justified. "You think Trayvon's going to make it?" the voice from the stage asked.

Glaurea snorted, "Not if these line notes are proof of anything."

Thea groaned. She wished that she had been more on top of Trayvon when he had just been the understudy. If only she had pushed him to really get to know the part…Hell, if only she could have put up with Mike. Then they really wouldn't be in this position. She stared up into the rafters of the old building and prayed to Dionysus or whatever gods of the theater still existed. *Please let this show be good.*

It had been twenty years since Thea had acted. She had tried to make a career of it after college but couldn't quite cut it. There had been too many big personalities for her to stand out. So she left. Since then the closest she had come was teaching <u>Romeo and Juliet</u> to her high school sophomores. That was how the producers of this show had found out about her. They were in need of a director and she was familiar with the script. Was she interested? Without giving it much thought Thea had said yes.

Now here she was, lying in the middle of the stage and praying to long forgotten gods with the chance that they could avert the disaster that was about to take place tomorrow night. She didn't have a hope in the world. She spread her arms above her head and slowly waved them back and forth along with her legs, making an angel from her notes. It had about as much effect as reading them did.

Glaurea glanced up at the stage when she heard the ruffling of papers and sighed. She was going to have to print off *another* script for the director. She looked back down to the computer where she had switched from line notes to technical notes. Yet again, she was sending off an email about the unpainted stage and yet again, she knew it would go unread. The technical crew had all been at that night's rehearsal and had heard Thea's exasperated sighs for themselves. Yet still it was her job. So Glaurea dutifully typed up another long email enumerating every single thing that needed to change before tomorrow's performance.

Eventually though, there were no more emails to write. Glaurea closed her computer with a thud that echoed through the cavernous space. Thea was still prone in the middle of the stage. To Glaurea, she looked like a child who had fallen asleep in the middle of play; her willowy limbs thrust out from her while her long brown hair lay tangled with her script. "Uh, Thea?" Glaurea called softly, half hoping that the woman wouldn't respond. "I'm done for the night."

"Alright," the voice was quiet, as if the speaker was far away.

"Okay, well I think I'm going to go home. You good?"

"Go ahead, I'm going to stay awhile. I'll lock up, don't worry."

Glaurea paused for a moment, drawn between crawling up onto the stage beside her friend and heading for the door. She could tell that Thea was not in a good way. Maybe she should try to make her go home? But no, Thea was a big girl. She could take care of herself. Besides, everything would work out in the end. It always did. "Okay. Well, g'night."

"'night," that small lonely voice called back.

When Thea heard the heavy doors of the theater bounce against their frames she closed her eyes, basking in the feeling of being alone in the vast space. The stage lights were warm against her eyelids. There was an old theater rumor that if you lay in those lights long enough, you could actually get a tan. She wondered if this was true as she let her body relax, trying to let her mind go with it. There was little that was more calming to her than lying underneath those lights in the middle of the stage. Maybe it was the smell: the dry aroma of dust burning up under the lights mixed with the slight tang of sweat from the earlier rehearsal. It was the smell of her childhood, of the

Night is Over and Day is Almost Here

magic of theater where anything was possible. She breathed it in deeply. In and out, in and out. She was not asleep (though if Glaurea had still been there she might disagree) but in a state of zen. It was as if basking in the warmth and the dust was allowing her to let go of her stress. Maybe, just maybe, one of the theater gods had been listening. It was all going to be okay. Somehow, someway, the show would turn out alright. After all, that was the magic of the theater.

Sometime later Thea sat up slowly, feeling almost as if she had slept a full night's sleep. She was reenergized until she saw the mess of her notes spread across the stage around her. She let out a small sigh as she gathered the papers, noting as she did that her script was now completely beyond recognition. She'd have to ask Glaurea in the morning for a new one. She grabbed up her papers, not even trying to put them in order and shoved them in her bag. With one final look towards the stage, she killed the lights and made her way out of the auditorium. The doors boomed in the darkness behind her.

Her Peacock Feathers (as a Montague antagonist)
by Frank De Canio

No sportsman relishing a victory
against his foe in an athletic meet
would dish up such a large trajectory
of reportage. Yet she did who'd repeat
that some infatuated patron set
his heart upon her gender-bending role
in Shakespeare's Romeo and Juliet.
Forget her flaunting feminine control
as Romeo's ill-fated paramour -
that followed later when she donned a dress.
It was her rapier wielding overture
as Gregory that managed to impress
her fan, who having praised her cocksure guise
would serve as trophy that she'd advertise.

HISTORIES

Uneasy lies the head that wears the crown.

Henry IV, Part 2, Act 3, Scene 1

Understudy
by Elizabeth Sylvia

Shall I go win my daughter to thy will? – Richard III

I think of Elizabeth, Edward's daughter, that pretty box
for reconciling hopes. She never is onstage
except in the mouths of those who bid on her.
Here is a play with ghosts, two princes
locked in a tower.
                      Here is a play staged
in daylight, the stage boards inclining softly
like a woman would be said to move
towards an audience of shifting tastes.
And here is a girl who shares the name
of her mother
                      who was a queen
and wants this daughter to be queen,
though that life is a mouth of ashes
to speak her name with, this daughter
absent as an unworn costume
stuffed in the rafters
                            behind the stage.
An understudy earns her keep by learning
all the lines. Elizabeth can hang all day
closed in among the musty velvets
used, unused, waiting to be used again.
Three queens run
                  repeat on the boards:
the one whose husband died, the one
whose husband died, the one
whose husband died, but not before
he murdered her so she could reappear
in plaguing dreams.
                      Even the dead
want their stories to be told, are not content
the action should unfold without their curses
or their approbation. Everywhere language:
from the heckling audience,
                          the echoes
of these wars and famines whistling

through their bones, from the gallery above,
a procession of the dead calling death
for death, but nowhere calling, still as bones
hidden in the tower walls, as a mulberry
carried towards division in the womb, Elizabeth.

Cordelia's Wisdom for Today
by Wilda Morris

Repeated lines are from Cordelia
in *King Lear* by William Shakespeare

Time shall unfold what plaited cunning hides.
Ask Richard Nixon, "Who erased the tape?"
Who cover faults, at last shame them derides.

They're often drowned by elemental tides
while telling lies to make a clean escape.
Time shall unfold what plaited cunning hides.

Bill Clinton, too, found out how fate collides
with claims of innocence, how life reshapes
uncovered faults; at last shame them derides.

And Spiro Agnew learned when too much pride
makes men conceal their fraud behind a drape
that time unfolds what careful scheming hides.

Who's actions with his public face collides:
corruption, bribery, and even rape—
those covert faults—at last shame him derides.

Do not expect that goodness overrides
and gets you out of self-made wicked scrapes.
Time shall unfold what plaited cunning hides:
who cover faults, at last shame them derides.

Elevator Macbeth
by Maev Barba

My father was a Shakespearean actor. He played Macbeth.

My father is elderly and not allowed in New York. He was called on the phone by Maxine Doyle. We used an old telephone with a plastic receiver.
—is this Pat Barba?
My father held the phone and stood by the glass. We had a large window in the house. My father watched me for my eyes. After a deal of struggle, I affirmed.
—we have a ticket to Shanghai.
My father often wears his many rings, each representing a performance with his theater. They crackle against the telephone receiver, like many metal little spiders. My father's eyes have hollowed. His lips move like the birth of life at recognition, and then his eyes in an instant flash white like the heads of two trains.
—*petty pace, petty pace, petty pace*, says my father.

"Sleep No More", which premiered in New York City in 2011, is a production of *Macbeth* split between five floors in the New York, the McKittrick Hotel, 530 West 27th Street, New York City. "不眠之夜," which premiered in Shanghai in 2016, is a production of Macbeth split between five floors in the McKinnon Hotel, 101 West Beijing Road in the JingAn District of Shanghai.

"Audiences move freely through the epic world of the story at their own pace, choosing where to go and what to see, ensuring that everyone's journey is different and unique. Sleep No More features a cast of 30 performers. The show plays out across three hours in 90 cinematically detailed rooms ranging across the five floors of a vast disused building in the Jing'an district" (smartticket.com).

Guests wander at their leisure floor to floor, while each floor imitates a different scrap of Macbeth. Sleep No More is "deprived of nearly all spoken dialogue" (Wikipedia). "Deprived of nearly all spoken dialogue." What if it weren't? What if "Sleep

No More" were word for word? What if *Macbeth*, *Macbeth* itself, were split through five floors?

We arrived in Shanghai. My father found himself in a mirror and asked for my help. My father heard his own voice in a vastly empty room. I took my father in a cab and he could not take his eyes off his own fingers in his own lap. He has a ring for every Banquo. It is like he is grabbing a pile of coins. He does not understand if it rains on his head. Given his frequency for need of the bathroom, I have given him to wear beneath his charming corduroy trousers. I routinely hold his hands, though always doubtful whether they are clean. Moments of lucidity include: speaking into the eyes of a young black-haired porter, "Though bladed corn be lodged and trees blown down;" and to a woman frying meat, "Though castles topple on their warders' heads," and to a wall, a blank wall with nothing on it, around it or behind it, a wall of white, limitless proportion, my father stared and said, "Even til destruction sicken; answer me." He is seventy-nine years old, my father.

If the Shanghai production is split between five floors, then *Macbeth* would need to be split in five parts. There are five acts in *Macbeth*. Each act might be played on loop on each floor. Act 1; Floor 1. Act 2; Floor 2. And on. But these noir productions are split in an insanity between many rooms. You may enter at any time, shut your eyes at any time, plunge through the door at any time, slink away at any time. Actors on each floor must continually act out their fifth of Macbeth, must play simultaneously their own fifth from start to finish, running again and again, every twenty-four minutes.

If we went into each floor and watch each fifth of *Macbeth*, bottom to top, we would see the entirety of *Macbeth* in the order Shakespeare intended (only missing thirty seconds in between on your way up each flight of stairs). Two hours total, two hours standing, two hours wandering, completely disjointed: the murder of Young Siward, then the murder of Duncan, then into the murder of Banquo, then the death of Macbeth, then of Lady Macbeth.

I dried my father's head upon exiting the cab at West Beijing Road and led him into an awning of steam. There, I asked as to the entrance of the McKinnon Hotel.

Elevator Macbeth

Wikipedia: "Guests enter the hotel through large and (save for a small plaque outside) unmarked double-doors on W. 27th Street, and travel down a dark hallway, where they check their coats and bags. Giving their name at a check-in desk, they receive a playing card as a ticket and are ushered upstairs to a brief, dimly-lit maze. Many guests see this maze as the 'portal' back in time, for upon exiting they find themselves in a gaudy, richly decorated and fully operational 1930s hotel jazz bar, the Manderley. After a time, numbers corresponding to guest's cards are called. They receive their masks and file into a freight elevator, where their journey begins."

My father, entranced by the atmosphere of *Macbeth*, plummeted with more verve than I had known in thirty years, into the red and velvet of the McKinnon hotel and I lost track of him completely. I ran after him, scaling the stairs, seeing the production of actors in silence and spectators in Chinese, which my father speaks no word of. I plunged in after him, but was lost immediately to the blending shadows of Chinese fairy tales, noir, and *Macbeth*. My father, however, was completely at home. Whatever floor he travelled to in that time, I am sure, he blended in completely, maybe even overshadowed other Macbeths.

If the Shanghai production were not split by act but by scene, then we would need twenty-eight floors for twenty-eight scenes. Because Macbeth appears in seventeen of those twenty-eight scenes, we would need seventeen actors playing Macbeth, each acting his own scene on his own floor. There should be no actor Macbeth on floor one because there is no character Macbeth in scene one. Scene three, floor three: enter Macbeth.

Would we have enough space?
I consulted with a woman in the steam and found that there are at least ninety-four commercial buildings in Shanghai with over thirty-five floors:
-Shanghai Tower has 128 floors.
-Shanghai World Financial Center has 101 floors.

For the twenty-eight-floor, floor-by-scene production of Macbeth, audience members climb up to the seventeenth floor to see scene seventeen. And climb down to the sixth floor, to see scene six.

If the play were broken up by line, at 2,162 lines, we would require a skyscraper with 2,162 floors. If each floor is typically fourteen feet tall, this skyscraper would be 30,268 feet, or 5.7326 miles tall. Commercial aircraft fly between 31,000 and 38,000 feet, or about 5.9 to 7.2 miles high, so if we build the building for the floor-by-line production of *Macbeth*, flight patterns in the area must change.
The floor-by-line production of *Macbeth*, requiring one Macbeth per every floor playing a scene with Macbeth (60% of the total scenes), would require not 2,162 Macbeths, but 60% of 2,162, or 1312.64 Macbeths.

Would we have enough actors?
"The Year of *Macbeth*," 2018 in the UK, saw nineteen major productions of *Macbeth* in the major theaters and thirty-eight (including understudies) Macbeths. If we included all major and minor stagings of *Macbeth*, including high school and community theater, we might estimate upwards of a thousand Macbeths in the UK alone. Add Ireland's 2018 productions and we easily have two thousand Macbeths. Or consider all the Macbeths in other countries. Consider all the retired Macbeths, the fires of which we might reignite with this floor-by-line 5.7-mile-high production.
Why stop at the line? Why not go by the word?

There are 16,666* total words in *Macbeth*.
We need a building with 16,666 floors.
At 16,666 floors, that building must be 233,324 feet, or 44.1902 miles tall.

Doesn't this floor-by-word production interfere with air traffic?
The Karman line--at which scientists claim the earth's atmosphere meets the edge of outer space--is 62 miles above earth's surface. 62 miles versus 44 miles--The Karman line is still about twelve miles higher than the floor-by-line production of Macbeth.

And if the production were broken up by letter?

---

* This number, 16,666 words, does not count stage directions nor headings, nor dialogue attributions, i.e. it does not count "MACBETH:" or "FIRST MURDERER:" or "*exeunt.*" or "ACT I Scene II" and is therefore more accurate than what you will typically get with an online search, 17,121 words.

If the production were instead broken up by letter, the building would necessarily be 68,215 floors tall, as there are 68,215 letters in *Macbeth* contained within the words spoken by the players.

A "letter" in the floor-by-letter production of *Macbeth*, only includes letters within words intentionally produced by the actors in the production of the play. It does not count any characters in stage directions, in headings, punctuation, or in spaces. In this way, the line "LADY MACBETH: Out, damned spot! out, I say!--One: two: why," contains not 59 characters, but 29 characters.

So at 68,215 floors tall, the building of the floor-by-letter production of *Macbeth* would then be 955,010 feet tall, or 180.8731 miles tall.

We will then need an estimated 40,929 Macbeths (60% of 68,215), again, one Macbeth per floor per every floor playing a scene which includes Macbeth.

And the implications for the actors on each floor?
The actors must never move and must only utter one sound again and again as rapidly as they can. The actors will only appear to move as the audience members ascend because each floor will have the actors staged slightly differently floor-to-floor, in order to create an illusion of fluid movement in a play divided by many, many layers in time. For instance, if we begin at the beginning, we set the first floor with three players: FIRST WITCH, SECOND WITCH, THIRD WITCH.

The first floor contains only three actors: one to play FIRST WITCH, one to play SECOND WITCH and one to play THIRD WITCH. The second floor contains only three actors: one to play FIRST WITCH, one to play SECOND WITCH and one to play THIRD WITCH.

The three actors on the first floor, play the same three characters as the three actors on the second floor, same as the actors on the third floor, same all the way up to the 253rd floor.

Act I scene I contains 253 characters. The first and second lines, both spoken by FIRST WITCH: "When shall we three meet again" (25 characters, excluding space and punctuation marks) and "In thunder, lightning, or in rain?" (26 characters, excluding space and punctuation marks).

For the floor-by-letter production of *Macbeth*, in ACT I, SCENE I alone, we would need both the Oriental Pearl Tower

(153 floors; 1,535 feet) and Shanghai Tower (128 floors; 2,073 feet), leaving us with 28 extra floors for green rooms, coat rooms, reception rooms, etc.

For the floor-by-letter production of *Macbeth*, in Act I Scene I, we would need to employ 759 actors, 253 actors playing FIRST WITCH, 253 actors playing SECOND WITCH, and 253 actors playing THIRD WITCH. For all 253 floors, we need, set: a desert place; characters: three witches, effects: thunder and lightning.

For floors one to fifty-one, only FIRST WITCH speaks (see lines above), while SECOND WITCH and THIRD WITCH are present but silent.

For floors fifty-two to ninety-eight, only SECOND WITCH speaks, while FIRST WITCH and THIRD WITCH are present but silent: "When the hurlyburly's done," (22 characters, excluding space and punctuation marks) and "When the battle's lost and won." (24 characters, excluding space and punctuation marks).

For floors 99 to 123, only THIRD WITCH speaks, while FIRST WITCH and THIRD WITCH are silent: "That will be ere the set of sun." (24 characters, excluding space and punctuation marks).

Taking the very first line of act I scene I, "When shall we three meet again," we see that, on the first floor, the only character uttered is "W," while on the second floor, "h," the third floor "e" and the fourth floor "n."

The actor on the first floor playing FIRST WITCH will continually utter "W W W W W W W W," (phonetically the 'w' sound), while the actor on the second floor playing FIRST WITCH will continually utter "h h h h h h h h," (phonetically a continuation of the 'w' sound) while the actor on the third floor playing FIRST WITCH will continually utter "e e e e e e e," (phonetically the 'ɛ' sound) while the actor on the fourth floor playing FIRST WITCH will continually utter "n n n n n n n n" (phonetically the 'n' sound).

The actors on the first floor should be positioned almost in precisely the same way as the actors on the second, third and fourth floors, because one does not move their body much in the time it takes to say "When." But gestures move quite quickly.

Elevator Macbeth

I can move my hand from my belt to my eye in the time it takes to say when. In ACT IV SCENE I, "a cavern. In the middle, a boiling cauldron," the witches cast things into the cauldron. If each witch is able to cast Adder's fork in the time it takes to say "Adder's fork," then the Adder's fork will be thrown in over the course of ten floors. The movement, from grabbing to throwing, will be broken up into ten floors, each stage "a" "d" "d" "e" "r" "s" "f" "o" "r" "k" the witch's hand with the Adder's fork gets closer to the cauldron as the audience member ascends ten floors from "a" to "k."

If the audience member is capable of scaling four floors within the half-second it takes to utter "when" (phonetically 'wɛn'), and can continue this pace for the first fifty-one floors, he or she will hear, floor-by-floor, "When shall we three meet again / In thunder, lightning, or in rain?" though with slight modulation due to the words forming over the course of fifty-one different voices.

If an audience member maintained a steady rate up the stairs (say, ten seconds per floor), it would take them 682,150 seconds, or 11339.16 repeating minutes, or 189.48 hours, or 7.895 days to experience the floor-by-character production of Macbeth.

The idea of pilgrimage and trial is thrilling, but this experience, because of the audience member's travel rate, will wreck the play, or, I should say it more impartially, 'change the experience of the play so radically it cannot remotely resemble what Shakespeare had intended.'

What I mean is: If it takes ten seconds on average to scale one flight of stairs, then the first actor playing SECOND WITCH would need to utter the first 'æ' sound of "adder's fork" for twelve seconds, stopping her throat, breathing, and beginning again every ten seconds. To see just the chant then, "Double, double toil and trouble; / Fire burn and cauldron bubble," the character-by-floor production would need three witches on fifty-one floors times three because the chant is uttered three times. For this chant alone, the character-by-floor production would need one-hundred fifty three of each witch, or 459 actors split between one-hundred fifty-three floors.

If the audience member walks consistently at ten seconds per floor (without rest) for the entire 7.895 days of the floor-by-character production of *Macbeth*, he or she experiences *Macbeth* not as Shakespeare intended. But if the audience member sprinted at a rate of 8 floors per second, or 480 floors per minute, or 28,800 floors per hour, he or she could see the floor-by-character production of *Macbeth* in 2.369 hours, which would be about the average length, estimated between 2 to 2.5 hours, of a regular production of *Macbeth*, and every line would come out at a more or less regular speed.

There are two ways of achieving the floor-by-character production of *Macbeth*:
1. City-by-act scenario: we use the buildings available to us within a particular location with a high-density of buildings with more than thirty-five floors, such as Shanghai which, within just the ninety-five tallest buildings of Shanghai, there are between them shared a total of 4,712 floors. This is double what we need for the floor-by-word production of Macbeth, but only 16 percent of what we would need for the floor-by-character production. Because we are 24,088 floors short in this scenario, we would need to use another 803 of Shanghai's 30-floor average buildings. This or we split the floor-by-word production of Macbeth between five cities with high skyscraper (skyscrapers are buildings higher than 492 feet) density, e.g. Hong Kong (355 skyscrapers), New York (282), Shenzhen (270), United Arab Emirates (199), Shanghai (163). This then might be called the city-by-act, or act-by-city, production of Macbeth.
2. Space-elevator scenario: 68,215 characters, 68,215 floors, 955,010 feet high, the floor-by-character production of *Macbeth* would bring us 180.8731 miles higher than the earth's surface. Again, if the Karman line is 62 miles above the earth's surface, *Macbeth* takes us higher than three times the distance of the atmosphere. Audience members ride in an elevator (without a front door) within the 180.8731 mile high skyscraper and watch *Macbeth* in 2.369 hours. If the structure of the elevator permitted rows of seats, they could even sit down. If on average, each scene contains six players, and if there are twenty-eight scenes in *Macbeth*, then we can estimate the floor-by-character production of *Macbeth* will employ 11,460,120 actors.

The 180.8731 mile high staging of *Macbeth* will make it .07% of the way to the moon, which is 238,900 miles from the earth.

Hamlet, which is 4,000 lines, nearly twice as long as *Macbeth*, would then, in the floor-by-character production, reach to about .14% of the way to the moon. Together, *Macbeth* and *Hamlet*, if staged in this way, would read .21% of the way to the moon.

In the Globe collection of Shakespeare's theatrical works, the plays average 2,794 lines a play (since *Macbeth*'s 2,162 lines, are only 77% of the average length, each play would work out closer to 222.473 miles), or 222.473 miles, the floor-by-character production of Shakespeare's collected theatrical works (37 plays) would require a building something like 8231.501 miles high, or 3% of the way to the moon.

If audience members travelled at a rate of eight floors per second, or 112 feet per second, they would see Shakespeare's collected works 33.33 repeating times, simply by riding in an elevator.

The play-by-space production of Shakespeare's collected works (based on the floor-by-character production model) would employ, if each play contained an average of thirty-four scenes, six characters per scene, thirty seven plays, and 75,000 characters per play, would employ an estimated 566,100,000 Shakespearean actors per cycle.

As there are 33.33 repeating cycles (so, for simplicity's sake, let us say 33 cycles, while the .33 repeating may be a rest period, a history lesson, or an audio-recording of Shakespeare's sonnets), the entire play-by-space production will employ 18,681,300,000 Shakespearean actors, about 2.395 times the world's total population which, today in 2020, is 7.8 billion people.

If I put my father anywhere in the play-by-space production of *Macbeth*, he wouldn't need to remember any line, or any word or even the year he was living in. He wouldn't need my face, or his name, or his address or his coat. He wouldn't even need "out, out," or "brief candle." He would need only continuously, repetitively, eternally 'æ, æ, æ, æ, æ, æ, æ, æ, æ' or 'ə, ə, ə, ə, ə, ə, ə, ə.' How long would it take to find my father? I would have to spot him through the glass of the elevator, one in 7.8 billion Shakesepearean actors, one in 1.3 million Macbeths.

I found my father in the culminating orgy of the witches. He had made friends with the bartender. I rustled my father's shoulder and he said, "Heaven's breath smells wooingly here."

Calpurnia's Speech after Caesar's Death
by Chaitra Kotasthane

Antony spoke of honourable men, and I have come to do the same
Where have they all gone? Has the earth at their feet swallowed them?
For I saw not one standing by Caesar's side when he still breathed and his blood still sang
And even in his death, it seems, my lord is as friendless as he ever was

Woe, where art thou? Take me by my arm, I implore, and lead me to Hades' realm;
Perhaps interred in his orchards I shall find these men's judgment, for it has clearly fled them

Antony, honourable? I would spit at his feet
His eyes are red, but not from weeping,
Believe me when I say this:
I have seen the devil in them

On the morn of my lord's murder, I quaked with fear, for I had seen visions most terrible
And now? Oh, now I quake with a fear greater still, for the demons I have seen, they have escaped my dreams, and they are now prowling the Roman streets,
And the worst of them bears Antony's likeness

What honourable man barges into the house of a man freshly dead and tears his belongings from his grieving widow's chest?
Caesar's generous will was not Antony's to read;
He is devious scum and I shall treat him as such!

Cursed are those who live to see their progeny's death
Then what does that make me?
For Caesar's unborn babe was culled in my belly by the same men who murdered his mighty father in the Senate
Have you ever heard, countrymen, of an act so wretched?

Surely valiant Caesar deserves justice, both for his blood and his seed?

I demand it on my fallen lord's behalf - I am not his flesh, nay, I am something else:
I am the chalice he chose to pour his blood into
And I shall shield it with a wife's devotion and a widow's anger
I fear not the wrath of traitors, because I know, my friends, that your hearts are inflamed
And that every true man in Rome shall stand by Caesar's wife as she guards his wain

Antony Wrestles with His Love for Cleopatra: a Cento
by Wilda Morris

These strong Egyptian fetters I must break;
if I lose mine honour, I lose myself.
I made these wars for Egypt and the queen
whose heart I thought I had, for she had mine.
I must from this enchanting queen break off.
Would I had never seen her.

O, whither hast thou led me, Egypt?
I found you as a morsel cold upon
dead Caesar's trencher; nay, you were a fragment.
My heart was to thy rudder tied.

Let's have one other gaudy night.
The nobleness of life is to do thus.
Alack, our terrene moon is now eclipsed.
Thou, residing here, go'st yet with me,
and I, hence fleeting, here remain with thee.
This is a soldier's kiss: rebukeable.

Slow as the Elephant
by Elizabeth Sylvia

language-less, a monster – Troilus and Cressida

Athena loves Ulysses for his guile, Achilles for his prowess,
does not love quiet Ajax, though he grows
like a tree towards Olympus.
What patron will visit Ajax in his tent at night
and accompany the mammoth body, oiled and scraped,
as it wades towards the dark water of sleep?

Patron of the last child chosen in gym class.
Patron of the one who stands awkwardly by the swings.
Patron of the girl who lingers while someone speaks to her friend,
nervously cleaning her teeth with her tongue.
Slow as the elephant, both Greeks and Trojans call Ajax. Brainless, dull.
They say he carries his wit in his belly, his stomach in his head,
though Aristotle knew the elephant surpassed all other animals.
The deceptiveness of men's talk itches Ajax's skin.

Always there are those of us who drift slightly below the notice
of the gods.
Patron of the boy at the window, at the edge of the field.
Patron of the extra whose face appears eternally in the crowd,
of those waiting to be brought up from the minor leagues, from
the typing pool.
Patron of all those who have felt blood coursing the looping
roadways of the body
and readied, but for whom no opening has come.

PROBLEMS

The end crowns all,
And that old common arbitrator, Time,
Will one day end it.
Troilus and Cressida, Act 4, Scene 5

The Eternal
by K.B. Thomas

2122 Annual Conference
Shakespeare Societies of the Western World

June 11 - 14, 2122
Laughlin, NV
Golden Nugget Casino
24 Karat Conference Centre

Featured Papers:
Shakespeare: The Eternal Question: Cat Lover or Dog Aficionado? 5 Arguments in Favor of the Canine
    Guest Speaker, Hugo "Hotspur" Larke, PhD
    Sponsored by the Disney-Folger Library

Celebrating the Golden Anniversary: How the Authorship Question was Conclusively and Dramatically Laid to Rest in 2072
    Guest Speaker, Dr. Marjorie McPherson
Sponsored by CliffsNotes/Sony Corporation/23rd Century Fox

SSWW Congratulates the Winners of the 2122 Bottom Prize for Notable Theory or Research

Erogenous Zones: The Nape of the Neck in 'Coriolanus'; Cleopatra's Lips and Antony's Lascivious Wassails
    Dr. H. L. Bennett, Sapienza University, Rome

A Vindication of the Venerative Victorians, or, Think Not of them as Villains
    Hastings Wrede, University of Colorado

Shakespeare's Dark Lady: How Dark? A Look at Racism, Identity, and Presumed Mental Wellness in the Sonnets
    R. L. Arbuthnot, University of Sussex

Will's Last Will & Testament: Who Got the Best Bed? Sibling Rivalry, Sons-in-Law and Hamnet's Ghost
    Teresa McElhany, Heriot-Watt University, Edinburgh

The Best of Landladies: How the Real Mrs. Mountjoy Presaged the Fictional Mrs. Hudson
    Dr. Vince Brosofsky, Macalester College, Minnesota

Anti-Stratfordians Need Not Apply: A History of Pro Shakespeare Prejudice & Hiring Practices in Academia, 1950 - 2050
    Alexander Trimble, Wofford College, South Carolina

SSWW William Henry Ireland Scholarship Winners
(Presentations Saturday, June 13, 10am in the Beryl Ballroom
* Ticketed Event *)

A Word NOT Used in Shakespeare's Oeuvre: An Etymological Investigation of 'Tendril'
    V. C. Yoakum, Emory & Henry College, Virginia

Shame and the Fourth Folio: Authorship, Ethics, and the Greatest Cash Grab in Publishing History. The Plays of Wentworth Smith, 1601 - 1603
    James Lubbock Roy, Colby College, Maine

Throw Down the Gauntlet: Glove Making, Shakespeare's Father, and the Tercel in 'Troilus & Cressida.' Superfluous Evidence of Authorship from Shakespeare's World
    L. L. Marohn, Heidelberg University

Dromgoole Dramatic Award
Peggy Ward Carruthers will direct the Seneca (NY) Shakespeare Players in select scenes from The Royal Shakespeare's 1990 nude adaptation of *Richard II*.

Register Online: *ssww.org/Laughlin2122*

Conference Rates Offered at the Golden Nugget Casino; Coupon Code "Lear"

Families Welcome

When Shakespeare Wrote a Haiku
by Lynette G. Esposito

Morn at its bright birth
Brought light's sweet forthcoming hue
rejecting the dark.

A Bard and his Shadow
by Bogdan Groza

SHADOW: Why hast thou summoned me once more from peaceful slumber?

WILLIAM: I, summon thee? Surely you jest for ne'er once have I summoned thee. Thou appear'st from torpid shadows to test mine patience, a fickle figment of mine craft and nothing more.

SHADOW: Nay I say, nay. 'Tis thy craft that wills me into existence, that I hath explained time and again, but alas my words fall on deaf ears.

WILLIAM: Deaf they might well be, for time hast come and gone and through the windows of mine age I hath peered for far too long. Hark, hark, pensive phantasm! I need not your services this once, for these pages shall not see the dim light of the stage, only that of this brief candle. Out, out, now.

SHADOW: How now, just as our Cardenio? Tell, whatever became of that masterpiece that we worked so hard to complete?

WILLIAM: Relinquished into oblivion, ne'er to be seen by man's eyes or heard by their ears.

SHADOW: How so?

WILLIAM: 'Twas the story of another, not mine to write into existence. An old friend for sure, but one whom would not take lightly such an affront.

SHADOW: Then why, pray tell, hath thou called upon me on that somber night, to quill a story that was not yours to write?

WILLIAM: Again I reply, specter of my folly, that it is not I whom calls upon thee; thy presence merely emerges as I scribble the night away.

SHADOW: Let us leave hence that squabble for another time.

Now, why hast thou pricked all those words on papers and parchments on that faithful night the story of Cardenio and his not-so-faithful friend?

WILLIAM: To test my trade. I merely wanted to see whom was a better wordsmith, I or the Spaniard.

SHADOW: And who won this duel of wording wits in the end?

WILLIAM: Neither and both. Our means and ways are beyond compare and our ability to imbue thoughts into pages has no equal.

SHADOW: Ah, but I gather that the Spaniard has no specter at his side to surveil his scriptorium.

WILLIAM: That I know not, but do not dare to use such superior tones with me. I owe you nothing, thou are part of my plays by thy will, not mine.

SHADOW: Aye, I am not Ariel for sure nor you Prospero, though thou hast put all thy energy into that fine work.

WILLIAM: Aye, 'twas meant to be my final work, but others then followed. Alas, these pages shall be the last ones for sure. One note to end them all.

SHADOW: Ah yes, 'twill always be the final play with thee.

WILLIAM: Nay, 'tis the play outside the play which I have sought, the stage upon which shadows such as myself strut and fret their final hour. A stage which thy ghastly form cannot tread.

SHADOW: Thou should not use my words so lightly. I hath told thee of the stage of the world for it was something out of mine grasp, a reflection in a mirror I could only gaze upon.

WILLIAM: Lightly, you say? Thy words as well? Thou keepe'st thy role in too high esteem. Thou art a medium, I say, at best a whisper and an echo in mine ear. A petulant one at that.

SHADOW: Thy self thy foe, for thy hubris shall spell thy end.

WILLIAM: A spell perhaps, perchance an incantation of e'er-lasting life; so long my plays shall see the light of stage, so shall my name be spoken.

SHADOW: Meager consolation if opposed with Time's injurious hand; thou shall not know thy immortality, only thy humanly decay.

WILLIAM: Thou speake'st true and know'st no less but all, long ago have my pangs for mortal glory have been thwarted. There was a time for such a word, a yearning no other could comprehend, but no more.

SHADOW: Ah, I see that time indeed has transposed thy heart and mind for our bickering now is for mere amusement and not for an intimate search for answers. Swayed as thou hast been, thy self-made Olympus has crumbled, and you with it.

WILLIAM: Nay, I have descended on my own accord, finding mine own truths.

SHADOW: And you have always been both the sorrowful scholar and the sordid scoundrel, combining the best and worst of both worlds, colliding thy true reality with the stage's light and making them live together in harmony.

WILLIAM: Aye, old friend, for thy kind words I am forced to admit that thy hand hast had a great merit in such feats.

SHADOW: Now that the pleasantries have past, back at the task at hand: what will this final piece entail? A quarrel betwixt lovers, a story of mistaken identities, disguises and laughters or cloaks and betrayals? What hero of old shall I bring back to life, what historical figure dost thy quill require?

WILLIAM: Nay, specter of ambition, 'tis a work that far exceeds such trivialities.

SHADOW: You call me ambitious and you are an honorable man, but methinks thy parchments have already written thusly.

WILLIAM: As I have told thee, no countrymen shall lend their ears to this play and no kings of infinite spaces shall contemplate it. These words, written on a full moon night, will be all-encompassing yet ne'er present. They will be the fabric of mine life and thou, intertwined within these pages. We will use a language that has always been within us, one forgotten by all and still that is constantly changing. It will express all the sentiments man possesses, from the most base of them to the highest and noblest ones. I would you looked with mine eyes and see what we are bound to accomplish.

SHADOW: I see it, I see it well. Best start writing hence, morrow is soon to come and little time have we left. To end our words and start our scratching on the parchments, I will remind you one of the first lines we e'er written as one: since we came into the world like brother and brother, let us go hand in hand, not one before another.

Words Are Lies -- Magical Antidote #2

by Farnilf P.

Words are symbols
of other things.

This word tree
lacks real bark.

Fundamentalists,
dogmatists,
literalists,
densely misperceive
a direct relation,
an inviolable link,
between some
sole mental concept,
inspired by a word,
and an actual thing.

There is no literal truth.
A will never equal C,
much less be.

Words are lies.

Bards sing fair
of far fay glens,
and clerics growl fear
with resolute cant.
Though workers steer clear
when making the grade,
words are still symbols
of far different things.

For what is to me,
is different for thee.

If you did not claim otherwise,

I'd not be so blunt,
but truth is a noun and words are still lies.

Sure, our tongue may be common.
Noisy comms seem intact.
And always we parallax to abstraction
when peering point blank.
For palpable particulars
lay quantumly linked,
well past terms.

Words are lies.

The magician would have you know
incantations invoke Logos.
And sometimes it works, though,
of course, best, wed with science.

Words so employed might demonstrate power,
as those of bards or the state, by clan and from foe.
But before conflating a process with fabulized ends,
it's wise to recall, every combination of symbols --
calculating, controlling, mystifying, inspiring --
fails to capture the simplest apprehension
of nature's light play
in the woods.

Words fall flat, short,
lay trapped in small chambers,
where they're picked up by opportunists
for backstabbing gain.

Words delight and deceive,
spark love, holocaust.
With weak exegesis we forget,
feign certainty, lost.

Words echo in canyons,
ring tinny and die,
far from the roots
of the tree they described.

Words are lies.

A Feral Cat Named Shakespeare
by Lynette G. Esposito

He came to us in that odd way
A feline knows--
A porch seat empty,
An opened can of tuna on the step

His mind, a cat's mind, simply seeking
warmth and food.

This feral creature did not know
the generosity of a back rub,
the safety of a lap.
He became Shakespeare
who lounged atop my many books,
looked down upon me with wild feline
affection,
bit my toes in bed to play
and wrote a kinder story for my life.
With his clear instinctive sight,
he sees me better than I am
trusts me with his whole self,
not like a few words silent on the shelf,
but with a soothing purr.
Shakespeare warms my cold heart.

Shakespeare Replies to Attacks on Theatre
by Greg Bell

I.

Methinks you'll not say I exaggerate
In telling you that history repeats;
Full oft, I used my craft to contemplate
The many ways, o'er centuries, Time eats
Her own. And, certes, Caesar such a case.
The senate stamped him *praetor maximus*,
Unthinking the Republic to erase,
Yet Ides of March proved Time more ravenous:
Brought down decorum, brought the Republic down,
Down forum, down O magister divine!
And now, I hear some *populi* do frown
Upon the playing of these plays of mine.

The knife twists in my heart, *Et tu, Brute?*
Knew ye not from the start? *'Twas but a play!*

https://time.com/4823353/shakespeare-threats-julius-ceasar/

II.

Alas, diseasèd body politic,
What conq'ring worm defeats thee in thy prime,
What cursèd hand; and by what lunatic
Desire, by what new all devouring crime
Must thou now be beset? Oh, can it be
The caterpillar of the commonwealth,
With avarice, hath burrowed into thee
And, never sated, robbed thee of thy health?
Wise governance is put to exile hence,

The fattened worm feeds yet upon thy youth,
The lackeys of the state atop the fence
To gawp, like crows, and mock the saddened truth:
O comic accident, O irony --
They threaten those who play my tragedy!

III.

Grammercies, my friends, my lovers and
Mine enemies, that you assail me thus,
For that, from Lethe's sleepy mists, you sent
Me reeling through obscurity to dust
The cobwebs from my mind, still fevered now

With visions old of what we yet may be.
*(That man, proud man, should need be tutored how
His end could be the end of tyranny!)*
O send me forth, if you may conjure still,
If you would know the meaning of my verse,
And in our hallowed emptiness we'll fill
 The cup whose draught can ignorance reverse:
Fill then the cup with all humility
That, drinking deep, restores humanity.

Palinode: Shakespeare's Women
by Elizabeth Sylvia

If you watch a lot of tv, especially *critically
acclaimed*, you might come to suspect
that a woman is a pair of tits attached to broken,
a hurt circuit flipped again and again.
It's like we get written into believing
we are the worst thing ever done to us.
So I love how the women in Shakespeare
always say exactly what they think is true,
and are never only watery bags of damage
about to burst all over the scene.

When horrible things have been done
to them, they want revenge, but not
because vengeance is the only taste trauma
leaves living in their mouths. Revenge
is a word men use for women's restoration,
our way to imagine justice in the world.

In the comedies, they get their due and everything
returns to harmony with their uncorrupted souls.
And when it ends in tragedy, the women stumble
on through blood and destruction knowing
they witness to the wrong the world has done,
roaring that we are all more than would be made of us.

Me
by A.G. Angevine

There is no love in what I feel for you.
There is desire, pain, joy, and grief; no love,
Though longing squats within my chest, the old
Unwanted guest I never can evict.

Believ'd was I in love most of my life,
The subject of as hidden from myself
As one born speaking language dead to all
But those who pass'd ten centuries ago.

But now I know the difference between
My love and longing, twins made from two types
Of stone. When thorns are birthed between your lips:
"I think I fall in love with everyone,"

My wounded heart has barely strength to breathe,
"And yet you never fell in love with me."

You
by A.G. Angevine

The song is one we've known for years, and though
The words may come from you, I am the one
Who knows them all by heart. Your fingers dance
On vinyl strings, and my blood pumps in time

With every strum. How long did we see eye
To eye, and breath a single pair of lungs?
A shar'd eternity within a glance,
Kaleidoscoping moments into one.

You knew, by then, how much in love I was;
And still you held my gaze, across the room,
As though we did not sleep in sep'rate beds
And always would. And still I let myself

Believe one day you'd look at me and see
Things of which I never could be worthy.

The Bard Cowboy
by Lynette G. Esposito

Across the western plain
silence travels
one unsteady foot at a time
staggering, twisting, forward
until even the birds
stop their noisy chatter
to watch his coming.
The thirsty earth's dry tongue
avoids the travel- weary feet,
licks at the pathway puddles
but is not satisfied.

Silence comes.
Still.
Shakespeare stands, looks down…
writes his name in the dirt.

Bios

A.G. Angevine
A.G. Angevine is a queer writer and actor from the Pacific Northwest. She lives with two cats, two humans, and two very dramatic peace lilies.

Maev Barba
Dr. Maev Barba attended the Puget Sound Writer's Conference in 2018. She is a PNW native and a great lover of books. She used to sell books door-to-door. A doctor of astronomy, Barba looks into space and considers neither the small as too little, nor the large as too great, for the lover of stars knows there is no limit to dimension.

Greg Bell
Greg Bell writes because he must. A critical illness finally roused him to publish, 2013. He's since placed work in literary journals & anthologies and was 2019 recipient of the Kowit Poetry Prize. He's author of hybrid poetry collection 'Looking for Will: My Bardic Quest *with* Shakespeare' (Ion Drive Publishing, 2015) and two award-winning plays. He leads Green Poets Workshop at Beyond Baroque Literary Arts Center, Venice, CA.

Mickey Collins
Mickey ~~rights wrongs~~. Mickey ~~wrongs rites~~. Mickey writes words, sometimes wrong words but he tries to get it write.

John Davis
John Davis is the author of *Gigs* and *The Reservist*. His work has appeared recently in *DMQ Review*, *Iron Horse Literary Review* and *Terrain.org*. He lives on an island in the Salish Sea.

Dr. Thomas Davison
Dr. Davison has been teaching inside two state prisons in Ohio for the past five years. He has been deeply moved by his personal observations and interactions with his incarcerated students and motivated to create poems, short stories, and essays about their day-to-day lives and experiences. Thomas has recently created a not-for-profit Entrepreneurial Services for Felons (ESF). He has dedicated 100% of his writing profits to provide free one-on-one support services for felons and ex-felons.

Frank De Canio
I was born & bred in New Jersey, I worked for many years in New York City. I love music from Bach to Shakira to Amy Winehouse. I also attend a Café Philo in Lower Manhattan every other week, and a poetry workshop which are now, since Corona, ZOOM events.

RC deWinter
RC deWinter's poetry is widely anthologized, notably in *New York City Haiku* (NY Times, 2/2017), *Now We Heal: An Anthology of Hope* (Wellworth Publishing, 12/2020) in print: *2River, Event, Gargoyle Magazine, the minnesota review, Night Picnic Journal, Plainsongs, Prairie Schooner, Southword, The Ogham Stone, Twelve Mile Review, York Literary Review* among many others and appears in numerous online literary journals. She is also one of the winners of the 2021 Connecticut Shakespeare Festival Sonnet Contest, anthology publication

David de Young
David de Young is a completing an MFA with NYU's low residency creative writing program in Paris. He's the proprietor of a small independent publisher, Nordic Moon Press. He lives in Finland with his wife and two daughters.

Lynette G. Esposito
Lynette Esposito has been published in *Poetry Quarterly, Inwood Indiana, Walt Whitman Project, That Literary Review, North of Oxford,* and others. She was married to Attilio Esposito.

Robert Eversmann
Robert Eversmann works for *Deep Overstock.*

Anna Laura Falvey
Anna Laura Falvey (she/her) is a Brooklyn-based poet and theater-maker. In 2020, she graduated from Bard College with degrees in Classics & Written Arts, with a specialty in Ancient Greek tragedy and poetry. She spent her college career blissfully hidden behind the Circulation and Reference desks at the Stevenson Library, where she worked. Anna Laura has been a teaching artist with Artists Striving to End Poverty since 2019, with Lumina Theatre Company since 2021, and will begin a teaching fellowship with ArtistYear in January of 2022. She currently works as editorial assistant at *Bellevue Literary Review*, the medical humanities journal based out of Bellevue Hospital in Manhattan.

Kate Falvey

Kate Falvey's work has been published in an eclectic array of journals and anthologies, including the Mysteries issue of *Deep Overstock*; in a full-length collection, *The Language of Little Girls* (David Robert Books); and in two chapbooks. She edits the *2 Bridges Review*, published through City Tech/CUNY, where she teaches, and is an associate editor for the *Bellevue Literary Review*.

Teresa Sari FitzPatrick

Teresa Sari FitzPatrick is still trying to decide if selling books (Encore Books, Chestnut Hill, PA) or traveling the world was the better learning experience. She has an MFA from Rosemont College. Her poetry and essays have appeared in *Schuylkill Valley Journal*, *Cochlea*, and *Crazy Bitch* magazine. She served as the lead copy editor on the book *Answering Autism: An Integrative Plan for Autism, ADD, and Neurodevelopmental Delays*, written by the staff of Doman International where Teresa also worked as a teacher and French translator.

Bogdan Groza

I was born in Romania and am currently living in Italy; I finished my Master's Degree at the faculty of Padua and am currently doing a PhD in Philology and Literary Criticism in Siena. I have been writing since I was about eighteen and published short stories and poems in minor Italian anthologies; in 2019 I managed to publish my first book, *Athena*, with a small publishing company. I decided to also start writing in other languages to see how my stories change and in 2021 I published my first two short stories in English with *Deep Overstock* literary magazine.

James Hall

James Hall is a writer and medical professional working in Chicago with interests in cider craft, book collecting and mythology, his poems have appeared or forthcoming in, *Front Porch Review*, *Blood and Thunder*, *The Stratford Quarterly*, and others. He recently completed the manuscript for his debut novel *Canticle of Dreams*.

Ed Higgins

Ed Higgins' poems and short fiction have appeared in various print and online journals including: *Monkeybicycle*, *Danse Macabre*, *Ekphrastic Review*, and *Triggerfish Critical Review*, among others. Ed is Asst. Editor for *Brilliant Flash Fiction*. He has a small farm in Yamhill, OR, raising a menagerie of animals—including a rooster named StarTrek. As an AirB&B host on his farm he sets out a host of books ranging from poetry to fiction, including classical to contemporary authors.

VALERIE HUNTER
Valerie Hunter worked at her college library as an undergrad, where she occasionally read the new acquisitions when she should have been shelving. She now teaches high school English, and has read *Romeo and Juliet* more times than she can count.

CHAITRA KOTASTHANE
Chaitra Kotasthane is an aspiring poet, writer, and absent teenager. She is a regular volunteer at her school's library and enjoys contributing to various literary societies. She currently resides in Varanasi, India, and her work has been recognised by the Royal Commonwealth Society.

KARLA LINN MERRIFIELD
Karla Linn Merrifield has 14 books to her credit, including the 2019 full-length book *Athabaskan Fractal: Poems of the Far North* from Cirque Press. She is currently working on a poetry collection, *My Body the Guitar*, to be published in December 2021 by Before Your Quiet Eyes Publications Holograph Series.

JEN MIERISCH
Jen Mierisch's first job was at a public library, where her boss frequently caught her reading the books she was supposed to be shelving. Her work can be found in Fiction on the Web, Funny Pearls, Little Old Lady (LOL) Comedy, and elsewhere. Jen can be found haunting her local library near Chicago, USA. Read more at www.jenmierisch.com.

WILDA MORRIS
Wilda Morris, Workshop Chair of Poets and Patrons of Chicago and a past President of the Illinois State Poetry Society, has published numerous poems in anthologies, webzines, and print publications. She has published two books of poetry, *Szechwan Shrimp and Fortune Cookies: Poems from a Chinese Restaurant* (RWG Press) and *Pequod Poems: Gamming with Moby-Dick* (Kelsay Books). Her current projects are a book of poems riffing off science facts and theories, and a collection of poems playing with Shakespeare's words. Wilda's grandchildren say she lives in a library. Her poetry blog at wildamorris.blogspot.com features a monthly poetry contest.

SHAKTI PADA MUKHOPADHYAY
Shakti Pada Mukhopadhyay, BSC, CAIIB, DIM, DCO, MA (English), was an Executive in a bank. His writings in different social media have been reviewed with enormous applause. Three years back, a lyrical drama written & directed by him was staged with vast popularity. His writings have been published in a number of magazines like, *Borderless, Passager, Molecule,*

Better Than Starbucks, Tatkhanik, The Dribble Drabble Review etc. His writings have also been accepted for publication in the near future in some other magazines like *Muse India* etc.

JAMES B. NICOLA

James B. Nicola is the author of six collections of poetry: *Manhattan Plaza, Stage to Page, Wind in the Cave, Out of Nothing: Poems of Art and Artists, Quickening: Poems from Before and Beyond* (2019), and *Fires of Heaven: Poems of Faith and Sense* (2021). His theater career culminated in the nonfiction book *Playing the Audience: The Practical Guide to Live Performance*, which won a Choice award.

TIMOTHY ARLISS OBRIEN

Timothy Arliss OBrien is an interdisciplinary artist in music composition, writing, and visual arts. His goal is to connect people to accessible new music that showcases virtuosic abilities without losing touch of authentic emotions. He has premiered music with The Astoria Music Festival, Cascadia Composers, Sound of Late's 48 hour Composition Competition and ENAensemble's Serial Opera Project. He also wants to produce writing that connects the reader to themselves in a way that promotes wonder and self realization. He has published several novels (*Dear God I'm a Faggot, They*), several cartomancy decks for divination (The Gazing Ball Tarot, The Graffiti Oracle, and The Ink Sketch Lenormand), and has written for Look Up Records (Seattle), Our Bible App, and *Deep Overstock*: The Bookseller's Journal. He has also combined his passion for poetry with his love of publishing and curates the podcast The Poet Heroic and he also hosts the new music podcast Composers Breathing. He also showcases his psychedelic makeup skills as the phenomenal drag queen Tabitha Acidz.
Check out more of his writing, and his full discography at his website: www.timothyarlissobrien.com

FARNILF P.

Farnilf P. is a member of a pseudonymous arts collective dedicated to world domination. An ephemeral art book of this work is forthcoming from PiNPRESS.online, and the author is in negotiations with Evil Portent Publishing for a children's picture book edition.

KATHRYN PAULSEN

Kathryn Paulsen writes poetry, prose, plays, and screenplays. Her work has appeared in publications from Canada to Ireland to Australia, including *The New York Times, The Stinging Fly, Humber Literary Review, Scum, Spillway, Craft, Isthmus, Big Fiction*, and the *London Reader*, and she's received residence grants at Yaddo, MacDowell, and other retreats. She lives in New York City but, having grown up in a military family, has roots in many places. The summer after her freshman year in college, she worked as an assistant to the librarian of the Altus (Oklahoma) Air Force Base Library, where she first made the acquaintance of James Bond, thanks to a recommendation by one of the patrons.

DEBBIE PETERS
Debbie Peters is an attorney by profession, living in New York City, who can be found (Covid-permitting) wandering her favorite bookstores in the Big Apple. She dedicates her work to her beloved Gerson Lesser.

MICHAEL SANTIAGO
Michael Santiago is a serial expat, avid traveler, and writer of all kinds. Originally from New York City, and later relocating to Rome in 2016 and Nanjing in 2018. He enjoys the finer things in life like walks on the beach, existential conversations and swapping murder mystery ideas. Keen on exploring themes of humanity within a fictitious context and aspiring author.

ROY SCHREIBER
I've written about a half dozen biographies and character studies. For example William Bligh, the victim of the Bounty mutiny and other unexpected setbacks, has been a particular interest for a couple of decades. That interest produced two books, The Fortunate Adversities of William Bligh and Captain Bligh's Second Chance. It also enabled me to act as historical adviser and on camera participant in a British television program about Bligh.
Over the past couple of years, most of my creative focus has been on producing two plays, Happy Family and The Optimist, for radio/podcast. Happy Family is based on what happened to a group of working women in the 1970s when they sued a major corporation for equal pay and opportunity. Three NPR stations and a community radio station broadcast the show.
The Optimist is a satirical look at college professors. One campus radio station in San Francisco and one in Ontario, Canada broadcast this show. The HEAR Now festival awarded The Optimist their silver classification. Filling in the blanks in The Merchant of Venice occured to me after I read two plays, one good, the other not so good, that used Shakespeare's play in ways far removed from the original.

JOHN SULLIVAN
John Sullivan was an ACTF Playwriting finalist, received the 'Jack Kerouac Literary Prize,' the 'Writers Voice: New Voices of the West' Award, AZ Arts

Fellowships (Poetry & Playwriting), an Artists Studio Center Fellowship, WESTAF Fellowship; he was also a featured playwright at Denver's Changing Scene Summer Playfest, an Eco-Arts Fellow with Earth Matters On Stage, Artistic Director of Theater Degree Zero, and directed the Augusto Boal / Theatre of the Oppressed (TO) wing at Seattle Public Theater. He uses TO with communities to promote dialogue on environmental and climate justice with environmental health scientists. His work has been published in a variety of print and online venues. Weasel Press (Manvel, TX) published his first book, *Bye-Bye No Fly Zone*, in December 2019. *When Story Stops, the Leak Begins* came out from Unsolicited Press (Portland, OR) in April 2020. His collection of short plays and performance pieces, *Dire Moon Cartoons*, was just published (also) by Weasel Press on October 5th, 2021.

Elizabeth Sylvia

Elizabeth Sylvia (she/her) is a writer of poems and other lists who lives with her family in Massachusetts, where she teaches high school English and coaches debate. Elizabeth's work is upcoming or has recently appeared in *Salamander, Pleiades, Soundings East, J Journal, RHINO, Main Street Rag* and a bunch of other wonderful journals. She is currently working on a verse investigation of the writer Elizabeth Barstow Stoddard.

K.B. Thomas

K. B. Thomas has been a book lover and bookseller since dinosaurs roamed the earth. She works, writes, and walks her dog in Portland, OR. Find more fiction at: kbthomas.net

Z.B. Wagman

Z.B. Wagman is an editor for the *Deep Overstock Literary Journal* and a co-host of the Deep Overstock Fiction podcast. When not writing or editing he can be found behind the desk at the Beaverton City Library, where he finds much inspiration.

Nicholas Yandell

Nicholas Yandell is a composer, who sometimes creates with words instead of sound. In those cases, he usually ends up with fiction and occasionally poetry. He also paints and draws, and often all these activities become combined, because they're really not all that different from each other, and it's all just art right?
When not working on creative projects, Nick works as a bookseller at Powell's Books in Portland, Oregon, where he enjoys being surrounded by a wealth of knowledge, as well as working and interacting with creatively stimulating people. He has a website where he displays his creations; it's nicholasyandell.com. Check it out!

All rights to the works contained in this journal belong to their respective authors. Any ideas or beliefs presented by these authors do not necessarily reflect the ideas or beliefs held by Deep Overstock's *editors.*

CPSIA information can be obtained
at www.ICGtesting.com
Printed in the USA
FSHW010029231221
87136FS